PERILOUS RIPTIDE

LANTERN BEACH MYSTERIES, BOOK 5

CHRISTY BARRITT

River Heights

COMPLETE BOOK LIST

Squeaky Clean Mysteries:

   #1 Hazardous Duty

   #2 Suspicious Minds

   #2.5 It Came Upon a Midnight Crime (novella)

   #3 Organized Grime

   #4 Dirty Deeds

   #5 The Scum of All Fears

   #6 To Love, Honor and Perish

   #7 Mucky Streak

   #8 Foul Play

   #9 Broom & Gloom

   #10 Dust and Obey

   #11 Thrill Squeaker

   #11.5 Swept Away (novella)

   #12 Cunning Attractions

   #13 Cold Case: Clean Getaway

   #14 Cold Case: Clean Sweep

   #15 Cold Case: Clean Break

#16 Cleans to an End

While You Were Sweeping, A Riley Thomas Spinoff

The Sierra Files:
#1 Pounced

#2 Hunted

#3 Pranced

#4 Rattled

The Gabby St. Claire Diaries (a Tween Mystery series):
#1 The Curtain Call Caper

#2 The Disappearing Dog Dilemma

#3 The Bungled Bike Burglaries

The Worst Detective Ever
#1 Ready to Fumble

#2 Reign of Error

#3 Safety in Blunders

#4 Join the Flub

#5 Blooper Freak

#6 Flaw Abiding Citizen

#7 Gaffe Out Loud

#8 Joke and Dagger

#9 Wreck the Halls

#10 Glitch and Famous

#11 Not on My Botch

Raven Remington
Relentless

Holly Anna Paladin Mysteries:

    #1 Random Acts of Murder

    #2 Random Acts of Deceit

    #2.5 Random Acts of Scrooge

    #3 Random Acts of Malice

    #4 Random Acts of Greed

    #5 Random Acts of Fraud

    #6 Random Acts of Outrage

    #7 Random Acts of Iniquity

Lantern Beach Mysteries

    #1 Hidden Currents

    #2 Flood Watch

    #3 Storm Surge

    #4 Dangerous Waters

    #5 Perilous Riptide

    #6 Deadly Undertow

Lantern Beach Romantic Suspense

    #1 Tides of Deception

    #2 Shadow of Intrigue

    #3 Storm of Doubt

    #4 Winds of Danger

    #5 Rains of Remorse

    #6 Torrents of Fear

Lantern Beach P.D.

    #1 On the Lookout

    #2 Attempt to Locate

    #3 First Degree Murder

#4 Dead on Arrival

#5 Plan of Action

Lantern Beach Escape

Afterglow (a novelette)

Lantern Beach Blackout

#1 Dark Water

#2 Safe Harbor

#3 Ripple Effect

#4 Rising Tide

Lantern Beach Guardians

#1 Hide and Seek

#2 Shock and Awe

#3 Safe and Sound

Lantern Beach Blackout: The New Recruits

#1 Rocco

#2 Axel

#3 Beckett

#4 Gabe

Lantern Beach Mayday

#1 Run Aground

#2 Dead Reckoning

#3 Tipping Point

Lantern Beach Blackout: Danger Rising

#1 Brandon

    #2 Dylan

    #3 Maddox

    #4 Titus

Lantern Beach Christmas

    Silent Night

Crime á la Mode

    #1 Dead Man's Float

    #2 Milkshake Up

    #3 Bomb Pop Threat

    #4 Banana Split Personalities

Beach Bound Books and Beans Mysteries

    #1 Bound by Murder

    #2 Bound by Disaster

    #3 Bound by Mystery

    #4 Bound by Trouble

    #5 Bound by Mayhem

Vanishing Ranch

    #1 Forgotten Secrets

    #2 Necessary Risk

    #3 Risky Ambition

    #4 Deadly Intent

    #5 Lethal Betrayal

    #6 High Stakes Deception

    #7 Fatal Vendetta

    #8 Troubled Tidings

    #9 Narrow Escape

The Sidekick's Survival Guide

#1 The Art of Eavesdropping

#2 The Perks of Meddling

#3 The Exercise of Interfering

#4 The Practice of Prying

#5 The Skill of Snooping

#6 The Craft of Being Covert

Saltwater Cowboys

#1 Saltwater Cowboy

#2 Breakwater Protector

#3 Cape Corral Keeper

#4 Seagrass Secrets

#5 Driftwood Danger

#6 Unwavering Security

Beach House Mysteries

#1 The Cottage on Ghost Lane

#2 The Inn on Hanging Hill

#3 The House on Dagger Point

School of Hard Rocks Mysteries

#1 The Treble with Murder

#2 Crime Strikes a Chord

#3 Tone Death

Carolina Moon Series

#1 Home Before Dark

#2 Gone By Dark

#3 Wait Until Dark

#4 Light the Dark

#5 Taken By Dark

Suburban Sleuth Mysteries:

Death of the Couch Potato's Wife

Fog Lake Suspense:

#1 Edge of Peril

#2 Margin of Error

#3 Brink of Danger

#4 Line of Duty

#5 Legacy of Lies

#6 Secrets of Shame

#7 Refuge of Redemption

Cape Thomas Series:

#1 Dubiosity

#2 Disillusioned

#3 Distorted

Standalone Romantic Mystery:

The Good Girl

Suspense:

Imperfect

The Wrecking

Sweet Christmas Novella:

Home to Chestnut Grove

Standalone Romantic-Suspense:

Keeping Guard

The Last Target

Race Against Time

Ricochet

Key Witness

Lifeline

High-Stakes Holiday Reunion

Desperate Measures

Hidden Agenda

Mountain Hideaway

Dark Harbor

Shadow of Suspicion

The Baby Assignment

The Cradle Conspiracy

Trained to Defend

Mountain Survival

Dangerous Mountain Rescue

Nonfiction:

Characters in the Kitchen

Changed: True Stories of Finding God through Christian Music (out of print)

The Novel in Me: The Beginner's Guide to Writing and Publishing a Novel (out of print)

PROLOGUE
22 WEEKS EARLIER

AS CADY MATTHEWS paused outside the battered doorway, her heart thumped so hard in her chest, she feared she might pass out.

She was done. She couldn't do this assignment anymore. Couldn't lose her identity in order to bring down DH-7.

That meant she was going to have to step up and waste no more time in finding the information she needed.

If there was ever a time to take risks, it was today.

The environment around Cady grew more and more perilous with each turn. It was only a matter of time until Raul—the leader of the deadly gang—discovered who she really was: an undercover detective sent here to take the criminal enterprise down.

Cady stared at the door again, knowing that once she went inside, there was no turning back. Raul's lair lurked on the other side.

She knew Raul was gone right now, out doing something that was no doubt self-serving and illegal. He'd taken his key people with him.

Which meant this was the perfect time for Cady to go through his things and find what she needed.

If you're caught, you're a dead woman.

The thought haunted her. But how else would she get what she needed unless she took this risk?

The time was now.

With that affirmation firmly in mind, she slipped into his room, closed the door, and glanced around.

Raul's leather recliner stood isolated against the back wall. Remnants of last night's drug-enhanced party were scattered on the floor. Needles. Ghostly bags with a dusting of white powder. Beer cans.

The room smelled terrible. Like body odor. Urine. Sweat. Cady didn't even want to know what had happened in here. She'd avoided gatherings like these as much as she could.

She wished she could avoid this place now.

Before she lost her courage, Cady rushed through the room, toward a door on the other side.

Raul's office.

Cady had only been inside twice. He claimed this was his personal space, and that no one should step into the "Holy of Holies" without his permission. Mostly, it was Raul, Orion, and Sloan who frequented the room. But Cady hadn't seen Sloan in a week and could only assume he was dead.

She quickly picked the lock and slipped inside.

Instantly, the smell of Raul's expensive cologne hit her nose, making her eyes water. Her gaze adjusted to the dimness of the space. Glossy black walls. Surprisingly lush carpet. A heavy mahogany desk. No décor. No pictures. Just a computer.

Cady rushed to his desk and hit a key on his computer. The screen flickered on and demanded a password.

She'd only get three tries before the computer locked up. She couldn't take any chances. She might not get the opportunity again.

Cady pulled a special device from her pocket, something that the task force leader for this mission had given her.

"Please work," she whispered.

She jammed it into the USB port and watched as a box popped up on the screen, indicating it functioned properly.

This little device should help her to break the passcode and get into Raul's computer.

Sweat spread across her forehead as she waited, her heart pounding in her ears.

If Raul were to catch her he'd kill her—which he'd certainly do—it wouldn't be a fast death. No, it would be full of pain and suffering.

Cady had known that fact from the start when she'd taken this assignment. This was what she'd signed up for. What she'd agreed to. But it all seemed like a bad idea now.

She tapped her finger against the thick wood of his

desk as she waited. Why was this taking so long? Cady didn't have time. At any minute, one of Raul's henchmen could wander past here.

The sweat on her brow thickened.

Cady might be an undercover cop, but that didn't stop the fear from invading her. Her body was reacting to what could be the fight for life—a God-given instinct meant to keep people alive.

Her dad always said only fools deny their fear. Wise men acknowledge they're scared and push forward.

She didn't take much advice from her dad, but that was a good nugget to remember.

She needed to be wise. And she needed to finish this.

The little digital ball continued to spin on the screen as the program tried to work.

As she waited, Cady pulled open a drawer.

Nothing.

Nothing?

Did that mean Raul kept everything on his computer? She just didn't see him as the type to go totally digital. But he hadn't grown this criminal organization by being a dummy. He might look tough and street smart on the outside, but inside that street-gang-clothed body was a highly intelligent man. He had more business sense than Cady would have ever guessed.

That made him even scarier.

Finally, the ball stopped spinning. The computer's home screen flashed into view.

Cady released her breath as temporary relief flushed through her.

Quickly, she replaced the high-tech device with an actual jump drive. She needed to access Raul's files and copy them. The information would be illegally obtained—it wouldn't hold up in a court of law. But these files mixed with Cady's testimony would be enough to give the police the evidence they needed to put key members of DH-7 behind bars.

With DH-7 off the streets, the world would be a safer—and better—place.

And, in her own way, Cady would know she'd been a part of it.

Just as she inserted the jump drive, a sound in the other room caught her ear.

A door opened.

Her pulse jumped.

She had no time to get out of here—there weren't even any windows to offer an option. That meant, she had to hide.

She yanked out the jump drive and jammed it in her pocket, turned the screen off, and stood.

As she glanced around the room, a startling realization hit her.

There was nowhere to hide.

As the footsteps got closer, Cady ducked beneath the desk.

If Raul returned and came to sit here, she'd be a goner.

Please, don't let that happen. Please.

As soon as she uttered the silent prayer, a door opened.

Someone had entered the room.

CHAPTER
ONE

TODAY'S GOALS: FIX ELSA.
LEARN HOW TO COOK SHRIMP
SCAMPI. WATCH THE SUNSET.

CASSIDY LIVINGSTON LEANED against one of
the thick wooden posts that held her tiny beach cottage
high off the sandy ground. After giving Kujo—an
adorably sweet golden retriever with an unfortunate
name—a pat on the head, she sighed. She never thought
she'd get this much enjoyment from doing nothing.

Across from her, her neighbor Ty pulled apart her
ice cream truck, Elsa.

The bright pink truck with the hand-scribbled prices
had needed some work for a while, but with the busy
summer season, Cassidy hadn't wanted the vehicle to
be out of commission for too long. Labor Day weekend
had just ended, which meant that tourists here on
Lantern Beach would trickle back to their homes and
their jobs and bide their time until they could experience another vacation in paradise.

Cassidy's throat went dry as she watched Ty, and
she took another long sip of her lemonade. Her dad had

always been more of an inside person—a filthy rich businessman, for that matter. He paid people to do everything for him except get him dressed.

But Ty . . . he was another breed of man. He was handy, he didn't mind sweat or dirt, and he looked good throughout it all. Really good.

Right now, his white T-shirt clung to his defined muscles. A sheen of moisture covered his skin, screaming of hard work. His eyes looked determined and focused. The former Navy SEAL was inarguably the man of Cassidy's dreams.

She took another long sip of her icy lemonade.

"Can you hand me that adjustable wrench?" Ty raised his head just enough to project his voice through the humidity-laden island air.

Like a dutiful helper, Cassidy found what he was looking for in his well-used tool chest and brought it to him. "As you wish."

He breathed out a laugh and glanced at her. "You sound so compliant."

"I am." Her voice lilted teasingly.

"Of course you are." He chuckled again, not hiding his obvious doubt.

They both knew that Cassidy was stubborn and headstrong. As a detective in Seattle, she'd had to be both of those things at times. Then again, her life as Cady Matthews seemed so far away.

Cassidy kind of liked the new person she'd become —the laid-back, let-her-hair-down, enjoy-each-moment kind of person. Maybe it was who she'd always been but had never acknowledged.

Cassidy leaned into the truck, inspecting Ty's work even more closely. He'd removed the dash in an effort to figure out why the vehicle spontaneously began to play music—and usually at the worst times. Cassidy had been woken up many nights by digitized tunes like "My Bonnie Lies over the Ocean" and "Pop! Goes the Weasel." The last song definitely made her want to pop something.

"Well, what do we have here?" Ty reached into the depths of the dash and emerged with some kind of notebook. He stared at the leather cover a moment before handing it to Cassidy. "I'll let you check it out."

Cassidy inspected the outside of the worn pages. Yes, it was a book—of the journal variety, if she had to guess. Strange that it was found behind the dashboard.

"If I had to guess, the book was probably in the glove compartment at one time, and somehow it slipped between some crack, never to be found again," Ty said, as if reading her thoughts.

Cassidy leaned against the truck and opened it, expecting to see a log of gas mileage or ice cream sales or something practical.

Instead, she saw hand-scribbled words. And dates. And paragraph after paragraph of . . . commentary.

She squinted at the date on the first page. The journal had been started five years ago.

Flipping to the back, she paused. The entries had ended last October.

That meant . . . Cassidy's breath caught.

That meant that this journal had to belong to Elsa—the person, not the truck.

Elsa was the previous owner of the ice cream truck, the one whose body had been found in the vehicle. Apparently, she'd fallen, hit her head, and that injury had ultimately led to her untimely death.

A few months later, Cassidy had arrived in town and taken up ownership of the ice cream truck when Elsa's best friend, Ernestine, put the vehicle up for sale.

Cassidy's pulse spiked. She'd been curious about Elsa—the person—and had heard various tales about her around town. Elsa was obviously eccentric and lively, and she liked to have fun. Cassidy had felt a bond with the woman ever since she started driving the truck that was Elsa's namesake.

She started to read the first page from the notebook but paused and glanced at Ty. "Can I read this journal? Or is this too intrusive?"

"Whose is it?" Ty's head was still buried inside the truck as he fiddled with some wires.

"I'm nearly certain it's Elsa's."

He stopped working long enough to sit up and look at Cassidy, a knot forming between his warm brown eyes. "The previous owner?"

"The one and only."

"Well, she's not around anymore. It couldn't hurt if you took a little peek." He winked at her. "I won't tell anyone."

That was all the encouragement she needed. Cassidy opened the book again and scanned the first entry.

We have a naked vacationer here on the island. Goes and stands at his window every morning wearing nothing but his birthday suit. No one wants to see that freak show. Thou art not Mark Wahlberg. Or even his distant cousin, sir. Put some clothes on.

Cassidy snickered. She'd seen some strange tourists while on her ice cream route. But never a naked one, thank goodness.

She skipped to the middle, laughing at Elsa's observations about the town. She wasn't sure why the woman had chosen to write a journal about these things and keep it in her truck. But her stories were fascinating.

The next entry Cassidy landed on regaled:

Met a family today who couldn't stop talking about sea glass. They wanted to find sea glass. Blah, blah, blah. They even got their little girls to call it mermaid poop. How sweet. You know what I call it? Litter. People need to pick up after themselves and not send their trash into the sea, where delusional people will later glamorize it.

Cassidy had never thought of it that way.

Cassidy finally skipped toward the back of the journal. This was really what she wanted to read anyway. What Elsa's final entries were like. After all, some people believed Elsa hadn't died in a tragic accident and that she still haunted this truck.

Cassidy didn't believe in ghosts, but . . . the truck did exhibit very strange quirks sometimes—so many that the locals wouldn't even eat any ice cream from the vehicle, lest they be "cursed."

Cassidy skimmed the last entry and felt the blood drain from her face. She had to read it twice to make sure she hadn't misunderstood.

"Ty, listen to this." She straightened.

She must have sounded serious because Ty stopped working again and sat up, his full attention on her. "I'm all ears."

No, he was all heart wrapped in appealing muscles. She didn't tell him that, though. Not now, at least.

Cassidy began reading aloud. "I'm sitting outside the nature preserve. I like to come here and take a smoke. Don't tell Ernestine. She doesn't approve. Anyway, I saw a movement in the woods. I didn't think much of it at first, but then I realized there were two men out there. They were arguing, just like those two brothers from *The Avengers*. One of them forced the other one down one of the trails into the woods. Ten minutes later, I heard a gunshot. Only one man later emerged."

"What?" A knot formed between Ty's eyes again.

Cassidy kept reading. "I was going to leave. I was. But then my ice cream truck started playing a song. She's never done that on her own before. I took off as fast as I could. But I just know he killed that other man. But here's the other thing: the man who emerged was wearing a police uniform. And now I fear I may not make it to see my seventy-fifth birthday."

Cassidy and Ty exchanged a glance. Both of them

had suspected for a while that one of the officers here was involved with something shady. But Cassidy had been trying to keep her nose out of things and maintain a low profile.

"It sounds like Elsa was murdered, Ty." Cassidy looked up at him, a fire lighting inside her.

"I've seen that look before."

"What look?"

"The one that's usually a catalyst for getting involved with something otherwise forbidden."

"Being curious is forbidden?"

Ty stepped closer and squeezed her arm. "It's more important now than ever that you remain low-key. I came really close to losing you a few weeks ago, and I don't want to go through that again."

Even though Cassidy had changed her identity, a member of DH-7 had found her here in Lantern Beach and had come to collect his one million-dollar bounty. He was dead now—because of his own mistake—but that didn't mean this was all over.

Ty grabbed the sweaty glass of lemonade Cassidy had brought down for him and took a long drink.

"You and I both know there's a dirty cop in the area," she said. "We don't know the extent of what this person has done, but according to Elsa's journal it sounds like murder."

They'd both seen some suspicious activity near the lighthouse. One of the people involved had been wearing a Lantern Beach police uniform. And then there was the bomb that had been planted on a local ferry—a bomb that had been taken from the police station evidence locker. All that mixed with this journal entry verified their concerns.

"Maybe we should tell Mac and let him handle it," Ty said. "As the town's former police chief, he has a better knack for law enforcement than any of the actual law enforcement here on the island."

Cassidy's lips twisted, but she finally nodded stiffly. "You're right. Maybe we should tell Mac. I just have one question first."

Ty raised his drink for another sip. "What's that?"

"Where's this Preserve Elsa mentioned?"

CHAPTER
TWO

CASSIDY GLANCED AT the dense forest around her as she shoved another tree branch out of the way.

"Why haven't I ever been here?" Cassidy asked. "I mean, I've passed it a million times before, but never stopped."

The entrance to The Preserve had been unmarked—a gravel road through marsh grass. Cassidy always assumed fishermen and kite boarders used this area. It was truly a hidden gem on the island, though.

The waters of the Pamlico Sound stretched around them, lined by an expanse of sandy shores and weathered live oaks with exposed roots. On each side of the beach were marsh grasses, and bookcasing the whole scene was a maritime forest.

When she and Ty had pulled in, a family they'd seen had set up a colorful beach umbrella and cheerful folding chairs. Kids splashed in the water, a unicorn shaped inner tube floating nearby. A woman walked a hyper terrier, who curiously sniffed everything in sight.

A lot of people obviously knew about and enjoyed this area.

"It's a local's secret spot." Ty kept his gaze focused on the woods around them. "Waters are safer here soundside than they are on the ocean."

Safer definitely had its appeal, especially for families with young kids. "It's been a bad season on Lantern Beach with all the storms brewing offshore."

"And now we've got hurricane season on us, and every day it seems like there's a new rip current warning oceanside. Lifeguards had ten rescues last week."

"Sounds scary."

"People's natural impulse is to swim against the rip. Instead, you've got to swim horizontal to it until you're out of the current. Then you swim back to shore."

Cassidy glanced at him. His stained T-shirt had been replaced by a sky-blue Tee that warmed his skin and complemented his utility-style khaki shorts. "You ever been in one before?"

"A couple of times. Even for a Navy SEAL, it can get your blood pumping. Then again, surfers seek out those currents to pull them out into the ocean so they can catch a wave."

"One person's pleasure is another's peril."

"Unfortunate but true. I thought I would bring you here sometime. After tourist season ended."

"I guess we're right on the money then," Cassidy said. "Tourist season is done."

"I guess we are."

"Most likely, we're not going to find anything out here. Or maybe Elsa was a troublemaker and made all this up, and we're wasting our time."

"I guess we'll find out."

Warmth oozed through her blood. Having a partner beside her—with her investigations and just with life in general—felt amazing.

They'd been at this for ten minutes, and all they'd found were bugs, brutal underbrush, and a patch of unwelcoming wilderness.

Maybe this was all for nothing. What if Elsa had a vivid imagination? What if she'd been writing a book and this was some type of fictional entry?

Cassidy had to acknowledge the possibility that this was a wild goose chase. Yet something about reading Elsa's words got her blood racing. As much as she tried to suppress her investigative instincts, they were still waiting dormant inside her. All it took was the slightest whisper to stir them.

She'd use wisdom. If she and Ty did find something, Cassidy would step back. She had her boundaries—her life depended on them.

She knew Ty didn't want her to get involved in another possible crime in the area—he'd made that clear. But how could she not at least see if there was any meat to Elsa's story? Cassidy and that ice cream truck had become unwittingly connected since Cassidy had arrived on Lantern Beach, and she felt like it was her duty to find answers.

She glanced at the canopy of trees above them.

Besides, if there had been a body here, birds of prey and other wildlife could very well have decimated any remaining evidence.

Or someone else could have easily found it.

Yet there hadn't been any reported murders. Things like that were big news on a small island like this. In fact, they'd gone thirty years with no murders until Cassidy arrived on the shores.

So even though Cassidy wasn't here when all of this supposedly happened, certainly she would have heard about it. A discovery like that would have been the talk of the town. Or a missing tourist would have at least been reported.

"I think we should venture off the trail. If a cop hid a body out here, he'd be smart enough to conceal it far from the walking path." Ty slapped his neck as another mosquito pestered him.

Cassidy followed Ty, tromping through the thick, thorny underbrush. She was glad they'd decided to leave Kujo at home. Cassidy could only imagine the barbs and ticks his fur would have picked up.

Ty suddenly stopped and nodded in front of him.

Cassidy drew in a deep breath when she saw a snake sunbathing on a fallen tree, claiming its spot in a small patch of light that crept through the trees.

"A cottonmouth," Ty said.

Cassidy swallowed hard as she stared at the creature. "It's huge."

"We're going to have to go around."

Snakes. Ticks. Mosquitoes. Biting flies.

This was just one big, bad idea, wasn't it?

Ty skirted around the snake, his hand firmly guiding Cassidy. She kept her eyes on the venomous critter as she followed Ty's lead. The snake raised its head as it spotted them, its tongue slithering out.

Cassidy had faced a deadly gang before. She couldn't let a snake freak her out.

The truth was, she'd always been more of an inside girl. She hadn't exactly grown up going camping or hiking or exploring nature. No, she'd attended galas and political functions and etiquette lessons.

They continued deeper into the forest, looking for something that may not be there.

After an hour of searching, Cassidy finally paused.

"This was all for nothing, wasn't it?" She waited for Ty to agree, willing to admit this had been a bad idea, as well as a waste of time.

Instead, Ty slipped his arms around her waist and tugged her closer. "Time with you is never a waste."

She felt herself melt a little. Ty had a way of doing that. Over and over. Again and again. And it never got old.

He lightly brushed his lips against hers before murmuring, "But if we're done looking, we should get out of these tick-infested woods before we get Lyme disease."

"I love it when you sweet talk me like that."

"I try."

They exchanged a smile. They'd been dating two months. For the past month, Ty had known Cassidy's secret. He finally knew the truth about who she really was and what she was doing here in Lantern Beach, North Carolina. It had felt so good to get it off her chest. To stop hiding things from him.

But Cassidy knew that information could also make him a target, and she couldn't stand that thought.

For that reason, she was always on guard. Always watching. Always waiting for the other shoe to drop.

Trying to act normal with a million-dollar bounty on her head felt nearly impossible. If the wrong people found her again . . . she shuddered to think what might happen.

Ty took her hand, and they started back through the maritime jungle toward the trail. If a body was out here, it was apparently going to take more than the two of them looking for it. There was too much underbrush that needed to be moved. Too many snakes. Too much nature. Maybe the killer had known that. Had known this would be a perfect dumping ground.

Or maybe nothing had happened here at all.

As Cassidy stepped high, trying to avoid a tumble of weeds, her foot caught on something.

She stumbled forward, but Ty caught her.

"Whoa," he muttered. "Easy, girl."

She started to give a retort to the horse reference—which she knew was unintentional—but when she looked back, her words faltered.

A hand had tripped her.

A skeletal hand sticking out from the dirt.

TY STARED at the bony remains tangled in the thick underbrush. At one time, that hand had belonged to a living, breathing person. Now, all that remained was a skeleton. Beneath the vines and leaves and shrubby bushes, he could make out scattered pieces—a ribcage, skull, and humerus—that had been at the mercy of wildlife and nature for the past several months.

Could these remains be the person Elsa wrote about in her journal?

The situation seemed too surreal. It swept his mind back to his days in the Middle East. Each moment there was marked with so much death and tragedy. Ty had moved here to get away from it all—to find peace and to help others who had been in his shoes.

Yet Lantern Beach—in its underbelly—was turbulent. In spite of that, all that turbulence had led him to Cassidy, and he wouldn't change that for anything.

Cassidy squatted on the ground and used a stick to move some vines aside, so she could study the bones. She looked every bit the professional she'd once been. The laid-back beach girl was gone. In her place was the cool and composed metropolitan detective.

"If I had to guess, that's a gunshot wound right here through his ribcage," Cassidy said. "It would have hit his heart."

"Poor guy didn't stand a chance at being found out here. No one wants to tromp through this mess—except you."

"We can't call the police." Cassidy glanced up with a look of concern on her face. "What if one of them did this?"

"We can't *not* call the police." The situation was precarious. They'd both known that before coming into it. Then again, had either of them really expected to find a body? "Listen, let's call Mac and get him in on this. And let's take some pictures so we can have them as evidence. If there is a member of the Lantern Beach PD behind this, we need to have as many people involved as possible so it's hard to cover anything up."

Cassidy stood and nodded. "I like the way you think. I'll call Mac."

"I'll take pictures." Ty pulled out his phone and began snapping some surface photos. It was hard to see much because of the underbrush, but at least he'd have some sort of evidence.

Using his foot, he carefully moved some of the thorny vines out of the way and exposed more of the skeleton. He'd definitely guess this person to be a man, based on the size of the bones. A few rags still clung to the body, but most of the tissue and hair were gone.

Something glimmering beneath the body caught Ty's eye. Was that a bag?

He pulled a gum wrapper from his pocket and used it to carefully pick up the object.

Yes, it was definitely a baggie—a Ziploc. Something was inside. Business cards, it appeared.

"What is it?" Cassidy put her phone back into her pocket and knelt beside him.

As his gaze focused on the card on the top of the pile, his heart stammered a beat. "That's my name, Cassidy."

"Why is your name on a paper out here beside the man?"

"I have no idea." Ty squinted. The paper looked like it had been torn off something else, some kind of white cardstock. A menu maybe?

Was this man a veteran? Had Ty talked to him about Hope House?

Ty had given out his name a few times because of that, so he supposed that could be the case here. It was the only thing that made sense. The scrawl wasn't Ty's handwriting, however.

More than anything, Ty wanted to dig inside the bag and find out more information. He wanted to move the body and see what was beneath it. But he knew he couldn't do that. He'd mess up the crime scene. Potentially ruin evidence that could point to what happened and who had done this.

It wasn't a risk he could take.

But he didn't like how this looked.

———

Mac Macarthur, the town's former police chief, showed up fifteen minutes later with his friend Clemson. Mac was in his sixties, with a spry build that didn't quite match his white hair, beard, and mustache. He'd also become one of Cassidy's favorite people since she'd arrived in town, almost a father figure.

Doc Clemson was Mac's best friend, and he doubled as both medical examiner and town doctor. He had yellow-orange hair and deep wrinkles that reminded Cassidy, at times, of a shar-pei—a very lovable shar-pei.

It seemed a shame that everyone was here except the actual police. But since Cassidy and Ty didn't know who was involved, they needed to play it safe.

Cassidy didn't like the fact that Ty's name had been found near this man. Why would someone put business cards in a Ziploc bag? Had someone wanted to set up Ty? Because without the bag, the paper would have most likely disintegrated in the storms and humidity in the area.

The unease in Cassidy's gut grew by the moment.

Mac stared at the remains. "You have a nose for trouble, Cassidy Livingston."

She nodded, not bothering to deny it. "Yes, I do."

Mac knew the truth about her past also—only he and Ty did. But Cassidy wasn't going to tell him about Elsa's journal. Not yet, at least. She wanted to see how everything shook out first. Something internal told her to wait.

Mac still stared at the skeleton and shook his head. "I hate that Ty's name is in any way associated with this body, but we're going to have to call Bozoman."

Bozoman was his fond name for Police Chief Bozeman.

Cassidy nodded, knowing his words were true. It was just that seeing Ty's name in that baggie . . . it made her question everything.

But Cassidy believed in the justice system. Because of that, she had to believe the truth would prevail.

While Mac called Bozeman, Ty took her arm and pulled her aside. The tension stretched across his face made her gut tighten. Something was wrong, yet they hadn't discovered any new information. So what caused the change?

"What was the date on that last journal entry, Cassidy?" he asked.

"October 31. Why?" She didn't like where this was going. Cassidy wasn't sure what that destination might be—she only knew it wasn't good. "What's wrong?"

Ty pressed his fingers across his eyes—a thumb on one side, his forefinger on the other. "Maybe I'm over-thinking this."

"Overthinking what?" Concern ricocheted through

Cassidy. Ty wasn't the type to overreact—and that alone was causing her to want to overreact.

He glanced over his shoulder and lowered his voice. "There was a costume party down at the pier that night. The rest of the gang convinced me to dress up—that's usually not my thing."

"Okay."

"Anyway, Austin, Wes, and another friend decided to dress up like the Village People and sing 'YMCA.'"

"That seems totally out of character for you. But keep going." Cassidy tried to picture it, but her tough SEAL didn't seem like the type. It was good to know Ty could let down his guard sometimes.

He pressed his lips together before saying, "Cassidy, I dressed up like a police officer that night."

Everything went silent around her. Had she heard him correctly? Certainly she hadn't. "What are you saying, Ty?"

He shifted, glancing around them again before his gaze latched onto hers. "I'm not saying anything, except that if Bozeman puts that together, along with my name being found with the victim's remains, I just might be the perfect scapegoat."

Maybe Cassidy shouldn't show Bozeman Elsa's journal. Maybe the commentary would tip the chief off too much and cause him to draw inaccurate conclusions. Maybe it would put people in danger. People like her and Ty.

Her gut twisted.

Cassidy wasn't sure what she should do. The law-abiding side of her told her to be forthcoming, to not obstruct justice. But the side of her that wanted to protect her loved ones urged her to stay quiet.

At that moment Bozeman came lumbering down the trail. Cassidy was going to have to make a decision and quickly.

CASSIDY WENT BACK to her house, determined to stay out of things. Bozeman had gotten the information from Ty and Cassidy. The two of them told him they were just taking a hike.

Which they were.

But Cassidy didn't bring up the journal. She needed more time to think everything through.

Even more so she didn't bring it up now that Ty had shared about that costume party. The dates lined up. He wore a police uniform. And his name was found by the skeletal remains.

Cassidy would be lying if she didn't admit that she felt unsettled by all of those details.

Finally, Chief Bozeman had told them they could go and that his guys would handle it from here.

Ty had a meeting with someone about Hope House, the retreat center he was starting for wounded war veterans. A few people had volunteered to work on the house either for free or at a discounted rate. Since the place was a nonprofit, Ty needed all the financial support he could get.

While he did that, Cassidy grabbed her mail, poured some icy-cold water, and sat down to check out what she'd gotten. It seemed routine and boring and anticlimactic after everything that had happened. But she needed to take a breather and try to stop thinking in worst-case scenarios about how today would turn out.

As she ripped open a thick padded yellow envelope, she smiled at what she saw inside. A Day-at-a-Glance calendar.

Just like the one her friend Lucy had owned. Cassidy had found one online and ordered it.

Her friend Lucy had been murdered at seventeen, and her killer had never been found. Everyone assumed it had been a random stranger who'd broken into their home, shot Lucy, and left. The police hadn't been able to pinpoint a motive. A reason. An answer.

Similar to the JonBenét Ramsey murder.

But Cassidy had been haunted by the event ever since it happened. In fact, the tragedy had changed the course of her life. The softball scholarships she'd been offered were no longer appealing. Her father's pressure to take over his company was no longer effective.

No, Cassidy wanted to be a detective. She wanted to fight for justice for voiceless victims.

Like Lucy.

In her downtime after joining the force, Cassidy had reviewed all the facts of Lucy's case. Some of them weren't known to her until she became a detective. For instance, she hadn't known that Lucy's father had been a suspect. That fact had never made the news. But the police had looked into him.

However, Hiroto had been at work that evening and two coworkers had seen him. He'd been cleared, along with Lucy's mom and neighbors.

Cassidy stared at the calendar in her hands. She so badly wished she'd been able to bring the one that used to belong to Lucy. Lucy's parents had asked Cassidy if there was anything of Lucy's she'd wanted after her friend—their daughter—had died. Cassidy had chosen that calendar.

Lucy had loved it and even made handwritten notes on some of the days.

Cassidy treasured that keepsake and often referred back to it. She'd even memorized most of the advice given on each day.

Tears filled Cassidy's eyes as she looked through this replica now. Memories sprung to mind. Images of Lucy with her jet-black hair. She would sit cross-legged on her bed and talk about boys and how she wanted to play in a rock band one day, even though her parents wanted her to join the symphony. Cassidy remembered her friend's infectious laugh and the way she'd felt like the sister Cassidy never had.

There were very few people in the world who understood Cassidy. Not many people could relate to being the only child of parents who were so wealthy they were practically untouchable.

Most people would think it was a charmed life growing up like Cassidy and Lucy did. But, in truth, it was a lonely existence. In between the loneliness was an immense pressure to perform, to keep up appearances, to be another successful check mark for their parents on their list of goals.

Cassidy paused as she flipped through the days, skimming the advice on each page.

She stared at the day in front of her, blinking as she read the words.

The man who moves big mountains does it by carrying away small stones.

Her gaze jumped up to the date.

February 29.

That's right. Lucy had died on a leap year, hadn't she? In fact, she'd died on March 3 of that year.

But in Lucy's old calendar, this date wasn't present.

Why hadn't Cassidy ever noticed it until now?

Why would Lucy have torn out this page?

Cassidy leaned back into the couch, trying to wrap her head around the thought.

The whole thing could be a coincidence.

It was also a possibility that somehow Lucy's calendar hadn't included February 29. The theory seemed like a stretch, but it could have happened.

The third possibility was that someone else had torn it out. Maybe before giving it to Cassidy?

That would most likely mean Lucy's parents had torn out that date. But why? Why would they have done that?

Certainly the killer, after murdering Lucy, hadn't stopped long enough to do it.

Cassidy didn't know what the answer was. But the truth was that it bothered her.

What had happened on that date?

And the even bigger question: How would she even find any answers thousands of miles away and unable to expose her true identity?

———

Cassidy had just changed into clean clothes before Ty came by two hours later. She'd taken a break from everything long enough to shower and do a tick check.

She pecked his cheek with a kiss as he sat beside her on the couch.

"How did it go?" she asked, pulling her legs beneath her.

"This guy wants to volunteer to do the electrical work for us," Ty said. "He's a veteran himself."

"That's great."

Ty nodded. "It really is. Everything is falling in place."

He was building on to his cottage, and the first phase of construction was almost done. He was adding a second story to his house and elongating the back. Phase Two involved adding some tiny homes on the property. Soon it would be able to house five to eight veterans in need of a retreat

"I'm really happy for you, Ty."

He wrapped his arm around her, and Cassidy tucked her head beneath his chin. He smelled clean—like the forest after a rainstorm. His chest felt broad and firm beneath her, and she couldn't help but note how the two of them naturally fit together.

"Thanks," he murmured into her hair. "I couldn't have done all this without you by my side."

"Well, I'm glad I'm good for something."

He kissed the top of her head. "You are good for plenty of things."

Warmth filled her. Ty's easy company was just what she needed after a day like today.

"What's going on with you?" he asked. "Anything new since our earlier adventure?"

"I got a calendar I'd ordered in the mail today," she said. "One like Lucy's."

"That's nice."

Cassidy wished it was that simple. She told him about the missing day.

"Maybe you're reading too much into it," Ty said. "Maybe it accidentally got torn out, and there's no story behind it."

Cassidy shrugged. "I know that's a possibility. But it still bothers me."

"Maybe one day when all of this is over and done, you'll be able to figure that out." A hint of sadness tinged Ty's voice as he said the words.

Cassidy turned toward him and rested her hand against his jaw. "With you. I want to figure it out with you."

He leaned toward her for another kiss. "I'd like that."

Cassidy knew the uncertainty was still bothering him—the what-ifs of the future. She wasn't sure how everything would shake out. She'd left her life back in Seattle, and she didn't really care if she ever returned to it. But a lot of unknowns hung over her head. It was impossible to plan for the future.

She cuddled next to him again and grabbed Elsa's journal from the couch beside her. "I've also been reading this."

"Anything new?"

"Lots of interesting observations. But nothing else pertaining to The Preserve."

"You can let the police figure it out from here." Grimness lined his voice.

She wanted to cheer him up, but her own reality gripped her. "I think Chief Bozeman is becoming suspicious of me. I've had some kind of connection to too many of these crimes. I should have never gone there today—just like you said."

"Then that man—whoever he is—would have never been discovered." Ty squeezed her shoulder. "Now that it's done, just stay low-key. Don't raise any more red flags. There's less than six weeks until the DH-7 trial."

"I'm trying. But after finding that skeleton today . . ." It was hard to trust that the cops would give this the justice it deserved.

"Mac promised to be nosy enough for all of us."

Cassidy remembered his parting promise. "That's comforting."

"You know Mac. If someone needs to be set straight, he's the one to do it—and he'll have a great time in the process. The best thing you can do is chill out."

Ty's words were true. But one fact still remained. "That's so hard for me to do."

"I have faith in you." He paused. "And, since the shrimp scampi didn't work out, I brought an already prepared dinner. Would you like some?"

"Would I ever. What did you bring?" She'd smelled something savory when he came in, but she'd been too preoccupied with everything else to ask.

"One of those buckets with seafood, potatoes, corn, and sausage."

"Sounds delicious." Cassidy stood. "Let me grab some plates."

She started toward the kitchen when her doorbell rang. She quickly glanced at Ty before grabbing her gun. Ty trailed behind her as she approached the door.

She glanced out the window, anticipating the worst.

Bozeman.

It was just Bozeman.

The man had dark, wavy hair along with a round face, bushy eyebrows, and a wide nose. Because he was slightly overweight, she'd assumed at first that he was older. In truth, he was probably in his late thirties.

Cassidy slipped her gun into the waistband beneath her shirt and tried to shake off the law enforcement persona that emerged whenever danger—or potential danger—presented itself.

Cassidy pulled the door open and smiled. "Chief. I wasn't expecting you."

He didn't return her smile. "Is Ty here?"

Ty appeared behind her—although part of Cassidy wished she'd told him to run. Her instincts signaled something was wrong—really wrong. When Cassidy put everything together, she didn't like the picture that formed.

"What do you need?" Ty stepped in front of her, always her fierce protector.

"I need you to come down to the station," the chief said. "We have some questions for you."

"Questions for Ty?" Cassidy blurted. "What do you mean?"

Ty's hands went to his hips, and his jaw hardened. "What's this about?"

"I'd prefer to talk down at the station."

Ty's eyes narrowed as he examined the chief. "Is this about the body we found earlier?"

"It is. We've identified the victim, and we have some questions for you."

CHAPTER
FIVE

CONCERN SURGED through Cassidy as the chief's words settled in her brain. Taking Ty in for questioning? Bozeman's glare made it clear this wouldn't be a casual, friendly chat.

Cassidy turned toward Ty, pleading with him through her gaze. "Ty, you don't have to go."

Ty's muscles bristled, but his gaze remained unwavering and sure. She usually loved his confidence, but, right now, it scared her.

"I don't have anything to hide," he said.

At his firm tone, Cassidy knew she wasn't going to talk Ty out of going. He was certain of his innocence.

But would Bozeman be?

She needed a different approach to stop this. She turned back to the chief. "Do you have a warrant?"

"No, ma'am. At this point, we're simply asking for cooperation."

She grabbed her keys, her thoughts charging ahead

in fast forward. She needed to buy time, to think this through, to ask more questions.

There's always another way. A quote from Lucy's Day-at-a-Glance. Cassidy needed time to figure out what that other way was.

"I'll drive you," Cassidy announced.

Bozeman drew in a long breath, tension coming in waves from him. "I'd prefer to take him myself."

"You said you're not arresting him," Cassidy reminded him. There was no reason Ty couldn't drive himself there.

"That's correct." Irritation simmered the chief's gaze.

"Then I can drive him."

She didn't wait for Bozeman to respond. Instead, she took Ty's arm and pulled him outside, pausing only long enough to lock her door. She headed directly to the stairs, not giving the chief the satisfaction of waiting for instructions.

"You're not in charge here, Cassidy," Bozeman called behind them.

"I'm following the laws of the land," Cassidy said. "Unless you're arresting him, then he has a right to drive himself down to the station willingly to talk to you. We'll be calling a lawyer also."

They climbed into Cassidy's car and shut the doors. It wasn't until she hit the lock button that Cassidy let herself breathe. To think. To respond.

Ty's hand came down over her wrist, startling her back into the present. "It's okay, Cassidy."

"It's not okay. Nothing is okay about this." She swung her head back and forth, worst-case scenarios pummeling her. Ty was going to be charged with this crime, and it wasn't okay. There wasn't enough evidence.

But the way Bozeman handled things around here, it didn't matter. He was trying to prove himself, lest everyone think he was incompetent—which he was.

"Cassidy . . ." Ty's voice sounded tense and concerned—concerned for her. Not for himself.

She finally stole a glance at him, and, when she did, Cassidy felt her heart crumbling into a million pieces. She wished she was overreacting. But the bad feeling in her gut had gone from blustery to a full-out hurricane in a matter of moments.

Ty pulled her into his arms. "It's going to be okay. I didn't do anything wrong. They'll see that."

Cassidy remained stiff, refusing to allow herself to be comforted. This was her fault. She should have let it go after she read that journal entry. But she hadn't. "I'm not telling him what Elsa wrote."

"You have to."

She shook her head, her mind already made up. "No, I don't. Especially not if someone in the police department is in on this."

Just then, Bozeman stomped down the stairs, cast them a glance, and then climbed into the police cruiser. A moment later, he backed out of the drive and his taillights glowed red in the mirror.

"We need to think this through," Ty said. "In the

meantime, I'm going to call Mac. And then I may need to find that lawyer you mentioned."

"Maybe Mac can recommend someone. You shouldn't say anything to Bozeman without an attorney. He'll use it against you—especially if he's already deemed you guilty."

"I agree. You know I had nothing to do with this, right?"

Cassidy leaned forward and ran her hand along the edge of his face, soaking in his beautiful brown eyes—brown eyes that were troubled right now. "Of course you didn't. Bozoman has no idea what he's doing."

Cassidy had always felt that way, but now she felt that way with more conviction than ever.

"You drive," Ty said. "I'll make the calls. And we're going to get through this, Cassidy. Don't lose hope."

———

Ty sat in the interrogation room, waiting for his lawyer to arrive. The sanitized odor of the place, along with the dim overhead light and suffocatingly small room made his head spin.

He'd refused to answer any questions without a lawyer present, just as Cassidy had advised. She'd been a detective, so he wasn't going to question her wisdom. However, the concern in her gaze and the fact she had a bad feeling spoke volumes.

Mac had recommended an attorney, a man named Ricco Salvatore. The man had recently moved to the area, and Mac had seemed impressed by him. The bad news was that Ricco was expensive. Ty didn't know where he was going to get the money to pay for him, but he hoped this would be a short-term thing. The chief would see Ty had nothing to do with this whole fiasco and let him go.

Finally, someone knocked at the door, and a man with light-brown skin and short, dark hair entered. Ricco Salvatore. Probably in his mid-thirties. Cool, confident, and well put together.

He looked like the picture of success, at least.

The man held out his hand. "Ricco Salvatore. Call me Ricco. Even though I just moved here, I am licensed in North Carolina—just to set your mind at ease. Now, tell me what happened."

Ty briefed him on today's events, and a few minutes later Chief Bozeman came in.

Ty braced himself for whatever the man had to say. Based on his uptight demeanor and narrowed eyes, this wasn't going to be good.

"Can you explain to me your connection with this man?" The chief shoved a picture toward Ty.

Ty picked it up and studied the image. The picture showed a burly man with a shaved head and menacing eyes. He looked vaguely familiar, but Ty couldn't place him.

"I don't know him." Ty shoved the picture back.

"We have witnesses that claim you do. Cullum McGrath ring any bells?"

Ty paused as the chief's words rolled over him.

Witnesses? What did that mean? "This is the man whose body was found today?"

"We believe so." The chief watched him like a vulture eyeing an injured wolf.

"It's too quick to get a DNA test back—or even dental records." Cassidy had reminded Ty of that fact on the drive here, reminded him not to take any bait.

Bozeman scowled and ran a hand over his sagging jawline. "If you must know, we found his wallet. Of course, we'll confirm that this truly is Cullum McGrath. But his timeline matches everything we know. He disappeared from Baltimore, Maryland, almost eleven months ago."

"I haven't been to Baltimore in probably eight years," Ty said.

"He and his girlfriend were vacationing here in Lantern Beach," the chief continued. "We have witnesses that say you confronted him on the night he disappeared."

Suddenly, the memories began flooding back to Ty. Memories long forgotten, that didn't seem important or like something that would come up again.

And Ty realized just how guilty he might look.

Another shot of concern coursed through him. Bozeman must have sensed a vulnerability and decided to move in for the kill.

"Do you remember confronting Mr. McGrath at the party down at the pier on October 31 of last year?" Bozeman asked.

Ty glanced at Ricco, who nodded that Ty should answer.

"Now that you gave me some perspective, I do remember Mr. McGrath," Ty said.

A touch of satisfaction glinted in the chief's steely eyes. "What happened that evening, Mr. Chambers?"

"My friends and I were at a party down at the pier. I saw a man and his girlfriend arguing. The man was getting rough. In fact, he pushed the woman. I was afraid he was going to hit her, so I stepped in and asked him to back off." Even thinking about it made Ty's blood heat with disgust. No man should get away with treating a woman like that.

"Do you always step into the middle of strangers who are fighting?"

Ty clamped his lips shut a moment before answering. "Not always. But I'm not going to watch a man beat a woman and do nothing."

"Sounds noble of you." Bozeman said the words but didn't sound impressed. His mind seemed already made up. "How did he react?"

"Not well." Ty's jaw twitched. "He punched me in the eye."

"And what did you do?"

"I defended myself. I had to get him off me before his rage did some major damage. But then the crowd stepped in and separated us before the confrontation could escalate any further."

"And that was the end of it?"

Ty raised his head, refusing to give Bozeman any more satisfaction. "That was the end of it."

The chief glanced at some papers in front of him. "Someone said you stalked the man afterward."

Stalked the man? Ty ran a hand over his face. The chief had been very busy this afternoon tracking down these so-called witnesses with what seemed like ease. "I did not stalk the man. What I did was watch him and his girlfriend walk back to their vehicle. I wanted to make sure he didn't take his frustration out on her—make her pay for what I'd done."

"And after that?"

Ty clearly recalled the moment. "I went home."

He hadn't been into the party anyway, but his desire to be social had disappeared after the incident.

Bozeman grunted. "You didn't follow him?"

"I did not follow the man." A touch of anger invaded Ty's tone, but Ricco nudged him, as if reminding Ty to stay in check.

"Would you care to share how your name ended up on a paper in the man's possession?"

The image of the hand-scribbled words flashed back to Ty. "I have no idea. The costume party was the only time we interacted. And that's not my handwriting on that paper."

"Are you sure?" Bozeman leaned closer, not bothering to hide his delight in having the upper hand here. "Because I think some of the PTSD might have kicked in. You followed the man. Threatened him. Led him to The Preserve and shot him."

Ty's shoulders tightened. "Don't be ridiculous. I haven't dealt with PTSD in a long time. I wouldn't be here, trying to set up a center to help other people struggling with those issues if I did."

Bozeman's lips twitched, and he leaned back. "But you did have some violent episodes, did you not, Mr. Chambers?"

Ty squeezed the skin between his eyes again before glancing at Ricco.

"You don't have to answer that," Ricco said.

Ty lowered his hand, knowing he needed to defend himself. "I have nothing to hide. I did not get violent when I returned from war. I had nightmares. I started yelling in my sleep one night, and the neighbors called the police, worried that something was wrong. That's it."

"But we know how these things can play out. They can come out years later."

Anger burned inside Ty. Was that what the chief wanted? Wanted Ty to explode and prove his point? Ty usually couldn't be goaded. But he was on the brink of snapping now.

Ricco leaned forward. "I think you've asked enough questions. Are you charging my client?"

"We have enough to keep him here overnight—at least until we finish searching his house."

"Searching my house?" Ty said, his back going ramrod straight.

"Don't worry—we have a warrant."

"What could you possibly hope to find?" Ricco

demanded. "A lot of people saw Mr. McGrath that evening. There's nothing that points to my client as being the one who killed him. That note with my client's name was written by someone else—maybe someone who wants to frame him."

The chief held up an evidence bag with a slip of paper inside. "On the back of the paper with Ty's name? There was a note saying: Meet me at The Preserve at eight. Same handwriting."

Ty rushed to his feet. He'd never left that note. Never met with McGrath again after that party. "I didn't do this. And I didn't write that note."

"We'll see about that." The chief nodded to Quinton, who stood at the door. "Lead him to the holding cell."

CHAPTER
SIX

CASSIDY TAPPED her foot impatiently against the linoleum floor of the police station lobby. She didn't like being on this side of the law. No, she needed to be out there proving bad guys were bad and good guys were innocent.

Good guys like Ty.

"What's taking so long?" she muttered, looking at the time on her phone again.

Mac patted her knee. "Ricco is good. Just let him do his thing."

"How do you even know this guy?"

"He just moved here from New York after having some heart problems. He's not a nice guy, per se, and that's what you want in a lawyer—someone who will get things done and not be intimidated."

"I guess." She said it with doubt, even though she knew his words were true.

Cassidy rushed to her feet when Ricco stepped into

the room a moment later. The man was younger than she expected. Late thirties maybe? And he looked out of place on the island with his styled hair and fancy suit.

She quickly read his expression. Between his furrowed brows and tight lips, Ricco didn't look happy.

"Where's Ty?" Cassidy glanced behind Ricco and waited for Ty to appear.

He paused in front of them, a briefcase in one hand and an expensive watch that looked just as heavy as his briefcase around his other wrist. "They're keeping him here a while longer. My guess is that he'll be here overnight. Ty asked me to keep you up to speed on what's going on."

"How can they hold him still?" Mac asked. "On what grounds?"

Ricco scowled. "I'm not really sure how they interpret the law around here—not like where I'm from. But, apparently, my client had a confrontation with the victim on the night he disappeared. The chief claims that's enough to hold him."

What? Cassidy blinked, certain she hadn't heard correctly.

"Is he being charged?" Mac asked.

"Not yet. But they have a search warrant, and there's an officer at Ty's house now looking for more evidence."

Cassidy felt herself deflating at the news. What a nightmare. Was this really happening?

"How is he?" she asked, hating the vulnerability that crept through her voice.

Ricco's face twitched, and he rolled his neck. But his eyes never lost their professional aloofness. "He's upset, as you can imagine. But he's fine."

"I need to see him." Cassidy glanced around, and her gaze fell on the chief leaving from the back hallway. Before her good sense could kick in, she charged toward him. "You have no right to hold Ty, and you know it."

Bozeman's icy glare met hers with a challenge of his own. "Careful, or I'll lock you up too."

His words didn't intimidate her. "How did you possibly track down a witness so quickly?"

"Wheezer—I mean, Officer Leggott—just happened to be at the party that night."

Wheezer. Another cop. At the party.

Convenient.

"You're not going to find anything at his house, and you know it," Cassidy said. "You're grasping at straws here, especially since you've bungled your last few investigations."

His scowl deepened. "You're out of line, Ms. Livingston. And how do you know so much about investigations? Can you answer me that?"

Her guard went up. Bozeman might not be the brightest bulb, but he was starting to put things together about Cassidy, wasn't he? She couldn't let that happen.

She raised her chin. "I read a lot of mystery novels."

"I don't buy it. There's more to it than that."

Her chin went higher. "You're right. I also watch *Law and Order*."

Bozeman leaned closer, not even a hint of amusement in his gaze. "I think there's more to you, Cassidy Livingston."

"I'm sorry to disappoint you." Cassidy sounded strong, but inside she quivered. It was more important than ever that she remain low-key. Yet her fighting instincts were clawing their way out. "I want to see Ty."

He didn't say anything for a minute. "You have five minutes. But if you do anything stupid, I'll arrest you too. Understand?"

Cassidy bit back all the things she wanted to say to the man and nodded. "I understand."

She'd be compliant . . . for now.

———

Cassidy's heart twisted when she spotted Ty behind bars in the police station's holding cell. She rushed toward him—he was the only one in there—and grabbed the metal rods separating them. Ty met her, his face ashen with worry that he no doubt wanted to conceal.

"Are you okay?" Her voice sounded airy and breathless.

He wrapped his fingers around hers, as if trying to reassure her. "I'm fine, Cassidy."

"They can't do this to you."

"They can, and they are. But Ricco says they won't

be able to charge me. They don't have enough evidence."

"No, they don't have enough evidence. But I'm not sure Bozeman is going by the playbook here. He's creating his own rules. Even if we take this before a judge, it could take a while to get you out of here. Oh, yeah—and the witness they have? It's Wheezer."

"Convenient." His eyebrows flickered up.

"My thoughts exactly."

"I'll be okay," Ty tried to assure her.

Cassidy glanced behind her, making sure no one was nearby. "If someone from the police department is behind this, you could be in a lot of danger, Ty."

"They don't know about the journal, though. Right?"

Her jaw clenched. "Exactly. And I'm not going to let them know. The person responsible will want to frame you."

"I can take care of myself, Cassidy."

Ty's words were true—he was capable. Cassidy had no doubt about that. Yet she still worried. Things could go wrong.

"I'm going to figure out who did this," she told him.

"You can't do that. You said so yourself earlier. You're on the border of blowing your cover."

"I'm not going to let you take the fall for a crime you didn't commit."

"The truth will come to light. If you blow your cover, you could die."

His words hung in the air. Cassidy wanted to argue. She did.

But Ty was right.

"I'll defer to Mac," she finally said. "But I'm not letting this go."

"I'm not going to be there to watch your back, and I don't like that. I know you're perfectly capable of taking care of yourself, but I feel better being there for you."

"I feel better having you with me also. But they're not going to frame you for this, Ty. I'm not going to let that happen."

"I don't see how they could do that. The fact that we argued and this guy had my name isn't enough to prove I'm guilty."

"Agreed. Without hard evidence, they'll be forced to let you go."

"Time's up," Quinton announced, appearing at the end of the hallway.

Cassidy leaned toward Ty, wishing she could reach him beyond these bars. But she couldn't. Instead, she extended her hand and stroked her fingers down his jaw. "I love you, Ty."

He took her hand and tenderly kissed it. "I love you too, Cassidy."

"Should I call your mom?" Her stomach twisted as the words left her lips. His mom lived in Texas and was going through chemotherapy. Her ovarian cancer had returned.

"No, definitely not." The firm shake of his head made it clear his mind was made up. "It will only worry her, and that's the last thing she needs right now. I'll tell her—but only if I absolutely have to."

"Okay. I get that. I'll play it cool."

But when Cassidy stepped back into the lobby area, she immediately saw distress on both Ricco and Mac's faces. Her apprehension rose so fast she thought she might drown in it.

"What? What did I miss?" Her gaze bounced back and forth between the two of them.

"The chief sent an officer to Ty's house to look for evidence," Mac said. "He claims he's found the gun used to shoot our victim. He says the type of gun matches the bullet."

CHAPTER
SEVEN

MAC TOOK Cassidy's elbow as he led her from the police station and whispered, "Keep a cool head."

Cassidy waited until she was outside to unload everything on her mind. The sun had long since set, and a few dimly lit streetlights didn't cut through the night-time around them. The only thing that seemed to offer any comfort was a breeze that swept across the parking lot. The slight chill helped cool Cassidy's warm face.

"He was set up, Mac," she muttered, still in disbelief that this was happening. She stopped by her car but didn't bother to get in. She had too much on her mind.

"I know. But getting angry isn't going to help anything right now. Let Ricco do his job, and we'll do our own investigation."

Cassidy pinched the skin between her eyes, her head throbbing. She couldn't deny the truth anymore. "I can't believe this is happening. It's all my fault."

"Why would you say that?"

"I insisted on . . . hiking." She couldn't mention the journal. "If we hadn't found that body, Ty and I would be eating dinner together right now. Instead, he's in jail."

"You couldn't have known, Cassidy."

She closed her eyes, remembering how Ty had discouraged her from doing all this. Why hadn't she listened to him?

She didn't explain further. There was no need. She knew the truth.

"I should have kept my nose out of it," she muttered.

"And let a murderer get away with it? It's not in your nature, Cassidy."

She finally raised her head. "What am I going to do, Mac?"

He pulled her into a fatherly hug, all his normal glib gone. "This is far from over."

"I know. I'm just so tired of everything being a struggle. Of making bad choices."

"You made the right choices—they were just the hard choices. You're doing the right thing, Cassidy. It's not always an easy road to walk, though."

The right way is often the hard way. Another quote from Lucy's Day-at-a-Glance calendar.

She wiped beneath her eyes. She hadn't realized the tears had leaked out, but they had. "Thank you. Everything is just getting to me."

"I'm going to see what I can find out from Clemson," Mac said. "Maybe he'll share something with me, let me know what the bones told him."

Cassidy drew in a deep breath and gathered her thoughts. She was done feeling sorry for herself. Now she needed to pull herself together and figure out a solution. "I'm going to call the gang and find out their version of what happened that night. I'm sure they were all together."

Mac studied her face another moment, his fatherly eyes warm and concerned in the moonlight. "You need me to drive you home?"

"No, I'll be fine. But thank you." It was a nice offer, one she was grateful for.

As soon as she climbed into her car—leaving a piece of her heart behind—she pulled out her phone and began making calls. Ty's gang of friends agreed to meet at Cassidy's place right away.

There were five of them—including Ty—that hung out on a consistent basis, and they'd all become friends of Cassidy's as well.

Austin was a contractor with looks that were TV home improvement show worthy. Out of everyone in the group, he was probably the one Ty was closest to.

Skye had a bit of a gypsy vibe to her and ran a produce stand out of a hippie van that extended into a pergola. Her niece Serena had just returned to Michigan for college a few weeks ago after spending the summer working at Lantern Beach.

Lisa owned her own restaurant called the Crazy

Chefette. She'd been a scientist before turning her career to creating crazy food combinations.

Wes was a plumber as needed and also a kayaking guide in the summer. He was the silent, deep thinker of the group.

When Cassidy pulled up ten minutes later, Austin and Skye were already in her driveway, standing beside Austin's truck.

"What's going on?" Austin straightened and took a step toward her, getting right to business. "Why are the police at Ty's place?"

Cassidy glanced at Ty's cottage, and her gut churned. Sure enough, a police car was in the driveway, and all the lights inside his house were on. Someone was still there, searching through Ty's things and looking for more evidence to frame him.

Since she'd seen Bozeman and Quinton at the station, she could only assume it was Wheezer here.

Had Wheezer planted the gun? Who else could have put it in Ty's house? Did the chief or Quinton have the opportunity from the moment the body was discovered until Ty was arrested? What if more than one of them was in on this?

A surge of anger rose in her.

"Everyone else should be here in a minute," Cassidy said. "I'm not sure I can explain this twice."

Just then, Kujo bounded down Ty's stairs, someone yelling after him. "Hey, wait!"

Kujo ran over to Cassidy and sat behind her, his

tongue wagging with amusement, like he'd been playing cops and robbers.

Wheezer stopped at the bottom of the stairs, his head jerking back with surprise. "Sorry. He got away. And I have a warrant."

The officer, whose real name was Billy Leggott, was thin and on the lanky side. Apparently, he had asthma and had earned his nickname because he constantly used his inhaler. It seemed an unfortunate name. But right now as Cassidy watched him gasping for breath, she could see why the moniker had stuck.

Poor guy.

Cassidy forced herself not to scowl. "I'll take care of Kujo."

Wheezer stared at her, his chest still rising and falling too rapidly. "You sure?"

"I'm more than sure."

He nodded and pointed his thumb over his shoulder and toward the steps. "Thanks, then. I best get back to work."

Five minutes later, the whole gang sat in Cassidy's living room. Between the wafts of the leftover supper Ty had brought earlier before everything turned upside down, Cassidy explained the events of the evening.

But each time she smelled the spicy Old Bay and the steamed shrimp and buttery herbs, her stomach clenched.

She and Ty should have been able to enjoy that meal. Together. And now she'd have to throw it all away.

Austin's face hardened until he resembled a bronzed statue. "I don't like this."

"Neither do I," Cassidy said. "Ty told me he was with you all that evening. Do any of you remember anything?"

"I remember that fight." Wes ran a hand across his shaved head. "That guy was angry, and anyone could see he was taking it out on his girlfriend. If Ty hadn't stepped in, I was going to. It was ugly."

"Had any of you seen this guy before?" Cassidy searched each of their faces.

Everyone shook their heads.

"There are too many tourists around here," Lisa said, hooking a blonde hair behind her ear. "It's impossible to keep them straight, especially since they usually change from week to week."

"What does this mean?" Skye asked, her big eyes round and full of concern.

"I think someone planted that gun in Ty's house," Cassidy said. "It wouldn't surprise me if someone planted Ty's name on the man, as well."

"How would they have planted that gun without Ty noticing?" Austin asked. "Has it been there for months, just waiting for this moment?"

Cassidy sucked on her bottom lip for a moment, considering her words. "No, I don't think so. My theory is that someone from the police department planted it there today after the body was discovered."

There was one person so far who had two connections to this crime: Wheezer.

He'd been at the costume party that night and had seen Ty.

And he'd been in Ty's house today, giving him the best opportunity to plant evidence.

————

The gang stayed another hour, offering moral support and trying to brainstorm possible scenarios about what had happened. And while Cassidy appreciated their efforts, she was no further along in discovering what had happened when it was all over.

And now the man she loved was behind bars.

Despite what Mac had told her, this all felt like Cassidy's fault. Even though she'd told herself she should find answers instead of beating herself up, she found herself doing just that.

How was she going to live with herself after what she'd done? In the past, her choices had nearly ruined her own life. But ruining the life of someone she loved? That was unacceptable.

She glanced out the window. Wheezer was still at Ty's house. More than anything, she wanted to march over there and give him a piece of her mind. But it was like Mac had said—outbursts like that wouldn't help the situation.

She dropped the curtain as her secret phone rang.

It was Samuel, her one and only contact from Seattle. He was the task force leader who'd helped her establish her new identity here. They hadn't spoken in a few weeks, and he usually called only if there was an update.

Part of Cassidy wasn't in the mood to talk to him tonight—not when she needed to help Ty. But she also knew if he was calling, it was probably important.

"Long time no speak," he said.

"I thought you'd forgotten about me." She leaned against the wall, still staring out the window.

"Never. The good news is that I've had no reason to call."

"Yet you're calling now." She couldn't help but point out the fact.

"Yes, I am." His voice dropped from lighthearted to serious. "I have a couple of updates I thought you'd want to know about."

"I'm all ears." The lights at Ty's place blinked off. She heard someone talking. No doubt Wheezer was going back to his vehicle and probably on the phone giving someone an update.

But what had he found? Anything else?

Curiosity burned inside her.

"First, I don't know if you've been keeping up with things on the news, but Ryan Samson was just elected prosecuting attorney of King County."

Cassidy's heart pounded harder at his words. At one time, she'd thought she was going to marry Ryan. Then he'd stopped calling or returning her messages. And when she'd met Ty, she'd realized just how dysfunctional her relationship with Ryan was. She'd called it off —one of her best choices ever.

"That's . . . uh . . . that's great."

"He's promising to move up the trial date," Samuel continued. "Which means you might be able to come back early."

"Even if I come back for the trial, you and I both know I'll never have a life there again." Cassidy had been in denial about that fact at first. But reality was kicking in more every day. Her old life was gone. Cady Matthews would no longer exist. Ever. There were too many people with a vendetta against her.

"With the gang leaders put away for life, you might have a chance."

"There will always be members of DH-7 who hate me. Even if I don't have a bounty on my head, I'll remain a target."

Samuel said nothing.

Cassidy knew why. There was nothing to say. Her words were true, and they both knew it.

"One more thing," Samuel's voice finally came back on the line. "You said Orion mentioned something about there being an unknown leader of the gang—one who was above Raul even."

"That's right."

"Unfortunately, we can't find any evidence of it."

Cassidy dropped her head and closed her eyes. "But it makes sense. Who's paying out this bounty? There's a puppet master behind all of this."

"If there is, he's good. We haven't given up, but it's not looking hopeful. I thought you should know." He paused. "One last thing. You asked if I could send you those business spreadsheets and memos that used to belong to Raul."

Her pulse spiked. "Yes."

"I'm not supposed to let you see them," Samuel continued.

The breath left Cassidy's lungs. Of course, she wasn't supposed to see them. She'd only been a small pawn in the course of things. Practically disposable, for that matter.

"I sent them to you anyway," Samuel said. "I had to drive two hours away and pay cash to mail it. But no one should be able to track that package and link you to this."

"You did that for me?" Samuel was a by-the-book kind of guy. That seemed unlike him.

"You've put your life on the line and on hold for all of this. I figured it was the least I could do."

"Thank you." Gratefulness filled her.

"I sent it yesterday. Expedited. It should arrive tomorrow. When we get off the phone, I'll text you an encryption code. And thank you for everything you've done. You at least deserve this. You haven't asked for much."

Cassidy slipped the phone back into her pocket and glanced out the window again.

Everything was calm and quiet at Ty's place— almost like nothing had happened.

Yet everything had happened.

Cassidy grabbed her favorite jacket—evenings could be chilly—and stepped onto her deck. Kujo followed behind her, faithfully sitting at her feet and panting happily. Having him here with her made Cassidy miss her own dog, Colombo, a German shepherd she'd adopted from a rescue group.

One of her coworkers had offered to take care of him before Cassidy went undercover. She missed the pooch, but knew he was well-loved and cared for.

She glanced up. The moon was breathtakingly big and bright tonight, and if Ty was here no doubt they would have gone outside just to stare at it. The orb hung over the water—over the mighty waves of the Atlantic—almost like a guardian from afar.

She leaned against the railing of her deck, trying to calm her scrambled thoughts. Having someone she loved in the line of fire had turned her little world upside down.

"I'm going to help you, Ty," she whispered. "If it's the last thing I do."

Just as the thought entered her mind, something on the other side of the sand dune caught her eye.

It was a man. Standing there. Facing her.

Cassidy's pulse jumped into overtime.

Whoever it was, he didn't bother to hide his presence.

No, he wanted Cassidy to know he was there.

But why?

CHAPTER
EIGHT

THE MAN not only faced Cassidy. He was *looking* at her. *Challenging* her.

Cassidy's police instincts told her to confront the man.

The survival instincts told her to hold back.

Cassidy fisted her hands, her entire body rigid as the decision warred within her.

Was this connected in some way with the dead body she and Ty had found earlier? Or could this confrontation be connected with DH-7?

Cassidy had no way of knowing. Not without going after the man and demanding answers.

As she stared back at him, her throat went dry. The man still watched her, clearly trying to send her a message. To intimidate.

Cassidy quickly ascertained his stats. Probably six feet tall. Broad. Based on his silhouette, he appeared to be wearing a jacket. In the darkness, Cassidy couldn't make out any fine details except . . . she squinted. Was he wearing a ski mask?

Cassidy couldn't be sure, but that's what it looked like.

Another shiver went down her spine.

She reached into her pocket, grabbed her cell phone, and quickly found Mac's number. She texted:

> 911. My place. Now.

Then she reached beneath her shirt and grabbed her gun.

If this guy was here because of the dead body at The Preserve, so be it. If he was here because he was a part of DH-7, that was fine also.

But Cassidy wasn't going to slink back inside like a frightened little puppy. She angled her face toward the man, more curious than ever.

Just then, the man took off in a run.

She couldn't let him get away. He might have the answers she needed.

Cassidy secured Kujo in her house—no way did she want to put her canine friend in danger. Then she darted off her deck to the stairs, across her driveway, and toward the dune. As soon as her feet hit the sand, Cassidy upped her speed and darted toward the spot where he'd been standing. Her muscles burned as she pushed herself to go faster.

But when she crested the peak, he was gone.

Gone gone.

She froze.

The man couldn't have disappeared that fast. He was around here somewhere.

She turned and scanned the shoreline. The open and expansive beach didn't offer anywhere to hide.

That left . . . the sand dunes.

Her hair stood on end.

Just as she was about to turn, the darkness tackled her.

No, *someone* tackled her.

Her body hit the sand with a hard thud. The man who'd been watching her straddled her midsection, his masked face hiding his identity. All she could see was the glimmer in his eyes.

"Stay out of it," he growled.

His grip on Cassidy's throat tightened, and she fought to breathe. She clawed the man's hand, trying to get him to let go. But it was no use. Using one last burst of energy, she jabbed her knuckles at his neck, catching his windpipe.

He released her throat long enough for Cassidy to rasp out, "Who are you?"

"I'm someone you don't want to mess with."

That voice . . . did Cassidy recognize it? She couldn't be sure. He spoke in deep tones, no doubt trying to disguise how he really sounded.

"You're not going to get away with this," she muttered, still struggling against him.

Whoever he was, the man thought he was invincible —and that only made Cassidy want to fight harder.

"Oh, you have no idea." He let out a chuckle.

She clawed at the sand, finally grabbing a handful of the grains. Using all her strength, she flung the granules at his face.

A moan escaped. His hands flew from her neck to his eyes.

Cassidy pressed her hands into the sand and scooted backward, trying to get away. Finally, she escaped the straddle hold he had on her and started to crawl from beneath him.

The man grabbed her ankle and jerked her back.

"Oh, no, you don't," he growled.

He raised his fist. No, he raised . . . a gun.

Cassidy let out a cry.

But there was no one out here to hear her.

Then something hard came down on her head, and everything went black.

———

"Cassidy, Cassidy! Wake up."

Cassidy heard her name in the distance, almost as if coming from another room. Or like someone was speaking into a glass bottle, and his voice wouldn't quite reach her.

"Cassidy!"

There the voice was again. She tried to find her way toward the sound. But darkness surrounded her. Blinding darkness that didn't allow her to see anything else.

As she took a shallow breath, another sound hit her. What was that? It was like something was crashing.

Waves. Those were *waves* crashing.

And they sounded angry.

Do something, Cassidy. Someone needs you.

Mustering all her energy, she tried to move. But she couldn't. Wait . . . her fingers moved. And they felt strange. Gritty. Dirty maybe.

The feeling returned to her face next. That same gritty texture greeted her like a backstabbing friend.

Where was she? What was going on?

"Cassidy." Someone shook her. Heavy breaths sounded over her. The darkness tried to fade.

She jerked her eyes open. Maybe.

The darkness remained.

No, that wasn't darkness. It was . . . sand. *Sand* surrounded her. Covered her face. Clung to her fingertips.

She heaved in a breath and nearly choked.

Her face was pressed in the sand, and the supple grains had molded around her features.

She pushed herself off the ground—only a couple of inches—and coughed. Spit. Wiped her skin.

A rush of memories hit her.

The man on the beach. Ty being arrested. The dead body.

How all of this was her fault.

That man had tackled her. He'd hit her with his gun. And . . . then what?

She shuddered, hating the unknown.

As someone said her name again, she turned onto her back. Blinked the granules from her eyes.

Mac's face came into view. His eyes—normally sparkling—were now filled with worry. Wrinkles Cassidy had never noticed before suddenly appeared on the angles of his face.

"You're about to give an old man a heart attack," he muttered, kneeling beside her and breathing hard like he'd just reached her. "I didn't think I'd find you. And then I did find you, and I thought you were dead."

"Sorry." She wiped sand from her face again and tried to get her bearings. She was on that sand dune near Ty's house. If she hadn't texted Mac . . . who knows when someone would have found her? "It wasn't my best moment."

Her entire body groaned as she shifted to sit up straighter. Her head ached with a pulsating throb that reminded Cassidy of her humanity. Her frail humanity. That had been tested one too many times.

But there was more . . . another ache. A different one. A slicing pain.

She glanced down and gasped at what she saw.

Something dark covered her shirt. Dark and wet and . . .

What . . .?

She was bleeding. On her chest. Near her heart.

Her head spun at the sight of it.

"We need to get you to the clinic." Mac took her arm, alarm written across his face.

Panic surged through her at the thought. "I can't do

that. They'll ask too many questions. They'll discover I don't really exist."

"You're bleeding badly, Cassidy. You don't have a choice. I can't fix this with butterfly bandages."

"But—" She wanted to argue, but her words failed her.

She glanced down again, bracing herself as she got a better look.

That man . . . he'd put an X mark over her heart. A clear message.

He was sick . . . and twisted.

He'd gone just deep enough to cause the blood but not deep enough to do much damage.

Mac slipped an arm beneath her and helped her to her feet. Everything felt like a blur around her.

"You should have waited for me," Mac said.

"You're right. I should have. I didn't want the guy to get away."

"He could have killed you."

Cassidy couldn't argue. She hadn't used good judgment, and it could have cost her life.

"Let's get you to the clinic," Mac said. "We'll do it on the down low."

She nodded, hoping Clemson would be there and keep this quiet. "But first I need to check on Kujo."

"I'D LIKE to keep you here overnight." Doc Clemson shone a light in Cassidy's eyes again as she sat in one of the rooms at the local clinic.

"I'm fine." Cassidy crossed her arms, hating that it had come down to this. But Mac had sneaked her in through a back door, and Clemson had taken her to the room at the very end of the hallway, where people hardly ever came.

The clinic was small and outdated, with only five rooms. The skeletal staff mostly treated minor ailments that didn't require a larger hospital, facility, or medical team. But the place was clean and ample and, right now, it was surprisingly quiet.

Which was good because Cassidy craved some privacy.

Doc Clemson had obviously been called out of bed. He wore Scooby Doo pajama bottoms and a sweatshirt.

Good friends are the ones you can call at any time of the night.

More Day-at-a-Glance wisdom.

Cassidy was so thankful right now for both Mac and Clemson. They'd both been there for her more than once.

"You took a nasty blow to your head. Someone cut an X over your heart. And you probably inhaled some sand. I wouldn't say you're fine."

She leaned closer, the stiff plastic mattress crinkling beneath her. "Look, my little secret is that I don't have money for this."

He remained unruffled. "I'll have you covered."

Cassidy swallowed hard, wishing the doctor didn't have an answer for everything. "The other secret is this: I don't want to leave any kind of paper trail that could let someone trace me here."

She held her breath as she waited for Doc Clemson to comprehend her words and draw any conclusions.

He paused from his examination and stared at her with perceptive eyes. "Why would that be?"

"I've made some enemies, and I can't let them find me." It was the truth—just without any details.

Doc Clemson grunted and put away his flashlight, tucking it into the pocket of his white coat. "Interesting. I don't like the sound of that. Did you report this attack to the police?"

She frowned at Mac, who stood in the background listening to everything. "No, I haven't. And I won't."

Clemson's eyes flickered with curiosity. "Why not?"

"Because not every police officer is as trustworthy as Mac. Besides, I have more hope of catching this guy on my own." Cassidy skimmed around the truth without telling everything. She hoped that would be enough.

"I have to agree," Mac chimed in. "I think it's a good idea to report this incident."

She sighed. She hadn't wanted to bring up the journal. She really hadn't. But they were leaving her no choice. They weren't going to give up unless she gave them a good reason to do so. "There's more to the story."

"There always is, isn't there?" Mac crossed his arms. "Go on."

Cassidy started to reach for her purse but stopped as pain sliced through the skin on her chest. They'd have to take her word that the book existed because her arm wouldn't reach that far right now. Besides, it wasn't that important that they see it with their own eyes.

"Could someone close the door?" she asked as voices drifted down the hall.

Mac did as she requested. With the three of them tucked into this room at the end of the hallway, she decided to share what she and Ty discovered from within the depths of her ice cream truck.

"Ty and I—mostly Ty—were doing some repairs on Elsa today," she started. "When Ty pulled out the dash, we found a journal. It was Elsa's, and it must have somehow gotten lodged between the glove compartment and the dash."

"Okay," Mac said.

"The last entry she ever added was on the night before she died." Cassidy glanced around. She had both men's full attention now. She drew in a shaky breath before continuing. "I can sum it up like this. On the day Elsa died, she saw someone in a police uniform at The Preserve. She couldn't make out who it was. But there was a fight, and the officer and the other man went into the woods. She heard a gunshot and only the officer emerged."

"So that's how you found that body!" Mac slapped his leg, as if he'd been sure there was more to the story.

Cassidy nodded. "I didn't know Elsa. I didn't know if her journal was accurate or if it was a work of fiction. So I wanted to investigate on my own."

"You didn't turn the journal in?" Disbelief stretched through Clemson's voice.

"I didn't. First, because Elsa wrote that she saw someone in a police uniform," Cassidy said. "But secondly, because Ty just happened to be dressed as a police officer for a party that evening."

Both men grunted. The sound made Cassidy's stomach clench. She knew how it sounded. How it looked. And she didn't like it one bit.

"I think we can all agree that Ty didn't do anything wrong here." Mac's face pinched in thought.

Cassidy let out her breath. She'd known Mac would be on her side, but it was good to hear the words leave his lips. "Correct."

"So, we can assume what I think all of us already know. There's a dirty cop on the force here in Lantern

Beach." Mac's gaze slid from Cassidy to Clemson. A glint of something was in his eyes. Satisfaction? Had he suspected this earlier?

Clemson and Cassidy both nodded.

"But Mac, the police have Ty in custody. If one of them actually killed this McGrath guy, they'll want to cover it up. They'll want a scapegoat. And that's why I'm afraid for Ty." Cassidy's voice trembled.

"I don't like this either," Clemson said. "Ty's in a precarious position—especially if the killer feels threatened."

"Also, someone left that gun at Ty's place," Cassidy said. "If this person is as dangerous as I think he is, he might even go as far as to stage something happening to Ty. An incident of PTSD where he had to defend himself and harm Ty in the process. I don't know. The possibilities are endless. And I don't like any of them."

"So, we need to figure out who really did this," Mac said. "And fast."

"Exactly." Cassidy turned to Clemson. "If you don't mind me asking, did you examine the remains?"

"I'm in the process. I had to treat a heart condition today and examine someone for a possible stroke. The living always come before the dead. I don't know anything yet, other than the man was shot through the heart."

"I understand." She grimaced as her cut throbbed again. "You did the autopsy on Elsa, correct?"

He nodded. "I did. But I didn't find anything suspicious. By all appearances, she fell and hit her head, causing an internal brain bleed. There was no sign of trauma, Cassidy. No bruising that would indicate someone pushed her."

"I get it." And she knew the chances weren't likely that Clemson could do more tests on Elsa. Cassidy was going to have to let that possibility go.

She turned to Mac. "I want to look into the officers on the force. I want to figure out which one is dirty."

The police force here was small with only three officers, including the chief. The receptionist also acted as a dispatcher. Apparently, when they needed more help, the state police stepped in. North Carolina also had a State Bureau of Investigation that handled many of the major cases.

"I'll help," Mac said. "I'll take Bozeman. It's less suspicious if I offer to have lunch with him. He won't appreciate the intrusion, but he'll probably say yes."

"Good point," Cassidy said. "That leaves us with Quinton and Wheezer. I don't know Wheezer very well."

"He's only a kid," Mac said. "Twenty-three. He doesn't seem comfortable with law enforcement and sticks with writing parking tickets and handing out speeding violations mostly. But he grew up here, so people like him."

"And then there's Quinton," Cassidy said.

"You should take Quinton," Mac said. "He's got a thing for pretty girls, so he'll warm up to you right away."

Cassidy had already observed that.

"Okay. We have a plan then. First thing tomorrow, we should get busy." Cassidy stood but everything wobbled around her.

Clemson nudged her back in bed. "You're staying here tonight. Off the books. But someone has got to keep an eye on you."

"Besides, you probably shouldn't go back to your place tonight," Mac added. "That man could come back for round two. I'll pick up Kujo and take him to my place for the night."

She wanted to refuse. But the men were right. Cassidy was better off here. "Fine. But first thing in the morning, I'm picking up where I left off."

CHAPTER
TEN

22 WEEKS EARLIER

CADY PUSHED herself as deeply as she could into the cave-like recess beneath the desk.

The door to the room opened, and her skin felt like it curled away from her.

Someone was in Raul's office. If she was discovered . . . she couldn't even think about it. Yet, at the same time, she couldn't *stop* thinking about it.

The footsteps crept closer, the old wooden floor in the room creaking like dry bones under the visitor's weight.

Cady held her breath and froze, unwilling to give her presence away.

Whoever was inside wasn't in a hurry. He'd paused. Only a thin sheet of wood separated Cady from the intruder, yet it was as if she could feel his presence invading her space.

Raul?

Her gut told her no.

Whoever was in here almost seemed to be scoping the room out.

Was it because he suspected Cady had come in here? Had someone seen her? Followed her?

A surge of anxiety gripped her, nearly choked her.

Death . . . in a way, she didn't fear it. In another way, it was a possibility Cady didn't want to face. She wasn't ready for it. Things in her life weren't lined up.

Did she even believe in the afterlife? In heaven?

She wasn't sure. And she needed to be sure. Those decisions shouldn't be made only when a person's life was on the line.

The person behind her took another step.

A step closer? Farther away? Cady wasn't sure.

Part of her feared feeling a bullet split through the wood above her. Feared an unseen attack coming.

Another step. Then another.

The person was coming around to the other side of the desk.

Cady's throat clenched tighter.

She'd given her life solely to her profession over the past few years. She'd hoped to have this investigation to show for it. Hoped to be able to say one day that she took down a deadly gang.

But other than that, what did she have to show for her life? No family. Sure, there were her parents. But she was such a minimal part of their life. She hadn't been important to them as a child, and she sure didn't feel important to them now.

Cady's best friend was dead, and she'd been reluctant to make more friends or to let anyone else get too close.

There was Ryan . . . but even the two of them had a strange distance between them. It was like they were together because they made sense more than because they were in love.

Was that enough reason to get married? Maybe. But was it the reason she *wanted* to get married?

Cady didn't think so. Nor was this the time to make those choices. Funny when your life was on the line what came to mind.

A shadow fell over the desk.

Whoever was in the room was in front of her now.

Cady dared to turn her head, ever so slightly.

Shoes.

She saw shoes.

They were black. Boots.

Cady squinted. They didn't strike her as the normal style that someone in DH-7 would wear. In fact, they were designer. And polished.

Strange.

The chair moved—just an inch or so. But Cady knew what was coming. She'd be exposed. Caught. Have nowhere to go and no backup.

She braced herself.

The chair stopped midway out. A squeal sounded behind her.

The door. Someone else had opened the door, she realized.

"Raul wants to meet with us," someone said. "Now. He thinks we have another traitor in our midst."

"I'll be right there," a deep voice responded.

The chair rolled toward Cady, hitting her leg.

The man on the other side didn't seem to notice. The footsteps departed from the room.

The door closed.

And voices filled the room behind her.

Cady released her breath—but only for a minute.

Because the truth was that Raul might suspect the traitor was her.

And the other truth was that Cady had no idea how she was going to get out of this room without being seen—and severely punished.

CHAPTER
ELEVEN

TODAY'S GOALS: PROVE TY'S INNOCENCE. FIGURE OUT THE REAL BAD GUY. STAY ALIVE.

FIRST THING IN THE MORNING, Cassidy hopped on her phone, thankful it still had some battery left since she hadn't brought her charger with her to the clinic.

Clemson had already stopped in once. He'd swung by the Crazy Chefette and picked up some savory oatmeal with parmesan, topped with an over-easy egg for Cassidy's breakfast. The combo hadn't sounded tempting at first, but Cassidy had practically inhaled the food. Now she craved more.

Clemson had also brought coffee with real cream— not the powdered stuff that they usually offered here at the clinic.

She owed the doc big time when she got out of here.

Cassidy's mind had been racing all night with everything she needed to do today once she was mobile again. She didn't have time to sleep or rest—yet she'd known the choice was ultimately good for her.

At least the clinic had been relatively quiet. Apparently, a college student had decided to go out for a midnight swim and had nearly lost his life due to the rip current. He'd come in with some scrapes and bruises. Other than that, she hadn't heard anything.

Now she needed to research this Cullum McGrath guy.

Social media was a gold mine when it came to investigating. People displayed their lives in digital snippets for everyone to see. The more people who saw the carefully crafted information, the more empowered the poster felt. What they didn't realize was that the more people who saw it, the more exposed they became.

Just as Cassidy had hoped, Cullum McGrath was no different. He'd proudly boasted his successes—and his rages—all over the Internet.

Cassidy cringed when she looked at the man's picture. He had icy hazel eyes, a thick neck and shoulders, and endless tattoos. He didn't look like the kind of guy you'd want to mess with.

But, of course, Ty had messed with him. The noble side of Ty hadn't allowed him to sit on the sidelines while a bully like Cullum threatened a woman.

Cassidy searched his pictures. Cullum hadn't posted in the past year, of course. Because he was dead. But his page was still up. Several people had asked where he disappeared to. There were no condolence messages, so news of his death probably hadn't gotten out yet. No doubt, authorities were confirming it was Cullum before telling his loved ones.

Several of Cullum's last posts were with a girl named Breena Munoz.

Cassidy needed to talk to her. Figure out who else may have wanted to kill Cullum. Find out what kind of activities—probably illegal—he was involved with.

The problem was that Cassidy couldn't leave the island and a phone call wouldn't do.

She'd figure out something. But right now, Clemson stepped back into the room to discharge her.

"Be careful out there," Clemson said. "This guy struck once. He could very well try again, especially if you don't heed his warning."

Cassidy nodded, all too aware of that fact. "I know. I'll watch out."

"Mac stopped by—you were still sleeping. He told me to tell you that he dropped Kujo off at your place. He's having an early breakfast with Bozeman and then he's headed up to Maryland to talk with some of Cullum's associates."

"By himself?"

Clemson let his head drop. "He's a former cop."

Cassidy backtracked. "I know. I know he's capable of handling himself. It's just that . . . backup is always a good idea."

"I couldn't agree more. He'll be checking in. I know he'll play it safe. You do the same."

Cassidy knew she needed to listen. Because, until she knew what was going on, it was hard to know whom to trust around here.

———

Cassidy hurried home and let Kujo out. When he was securely inside again, she took a quick shower and tried to clean herself up.

But when she looked in the mirror, she cringed. She not only had a bruise at her temple but also a huge goose egg. The stitches across her chest were uncomfortable and pulled every time she turned the wrong way.

But it could have been worse. She could be dead right now.

Cassidy didn't want Ty to see her this way. Yet if she didn't go down to the police station to visit him, he would know something was wrong. Besides, she needed an update on how he was doing. Had authorities formally charged him yet? If so, had they scheduled the arraignment hearing? Where did that even take place around here?

Things worked so differently in a small town—especially one this isolated. The whole keeping Ty without charging him thing, combined with the clumsy way they'd handled other crimes really got under her skin. But she wasn't in a position to act as an agent of change, so she'd tried to remain quiet.

Until now.

She used makeup to cover up what she could, and then she pulled up a high-necked T-shirt to cover her stitches. With her hair down, it almost covered up the knot on her forehead.

Cassidy frowned.

She was just going to have to do the best she could here.

She started toward the door when she saw the Day-at-a-Glance she'd ordered. Even though she'd just gotten the calendar yesterday, somehow it felt like months ago already.

She flipped it to the right day and read the daily advice.

Fight for those you love.

That was exactly what she intended on doing.

Grabbing her keys, she was out the door, and arrived at the police station ten minutes later.

Would she encounter her attacker from last night? She'd already decided that she would keep her head up and act as if nothing had happened. She wouldn't give whoever had done this the satisfaction of thinking he'd slowed her down in any way.

Quinton stood near the receptionist.

A smile lit his face when he saw her. "If it isn't Cassandra."

"Cassidy," she corrected.

He got her name wrong. Every. Single. Time.

He casually leaned against the desk, the dull expression gone from his face and a semblance of charm replacing it. The man was tall and fairly gangly with a protruding Adam's apple and sloppy grin that turned her stomach.

"What can I do for you?" He smiled, showing all of his pearly white teeth.

Cassidy offered a tight smile. "I need to talk to Ty Chambers."

His smile slipped, and he straightened. "It's not exactly visiting hours."

"You don't have visiting hours."

"We should."

"But you don't."

He glanced around, as if pondering the repercussions of his actions. "I suppose it would be okay. For a minute, at least."

"I appreciate it, Quinton."

"Follow me." He started down the hallway.

Was this her opportunity to get some information from the officer? She needed to take whatever chance she got. And that meant Cassidy needed to turn on the charm, even if it made her want to puke.

"Did you grow up around here, Quinton?" she asked, her voice sickly sweet. "You seem to really know this town."

"Nope. Grew up in Greenville but wanted to get away."

"So you got away to Lantern Beach?" Why of all places had he chosen this one? It wasn't high on the list of exciting places to be a cop.

"I did."

"It seems like an odd choice," Cassidy said. "You seem like the type who's destined for bigger things." Like being a car salesman at a small, not well-run dealership. Or a peon at a large corporation. But not a cop.

"True." He shrugged, his dopey expression

unchanged. "No, sometimes it's better to get away from bad influences, you know?"

"Bad influences?" What did that mean?

He shrugged. "I haven't always walked the straight and narrow. I know that's probably hard to believe."

"So hard." She tried to sound sincere. She really did.

He paused outside the door leading to the station's two holding cells, unlocked it, and stepped aside. "Ten minutes. That's all I can give you. Besides, the chief will be back in fifteen, and I'm not sure how he feels about this. Don't get me in trouble."

"You're the best, Quinton." She batted her eyelashes, promising to kick herself later.

His smile widened. "Thanks."

Cassidy stepped inside and braced herself to talk to Ty.

———

Ty stood from the uncomfortable bench he'd been perched on all night. He hadn't been able to get much sleep, so he'd finally given up. Instead, he'd let his thoughts turn over and over again. And he'd prayed— he'd prayed hard.

Whatever was going on here, it had the potential to drastically change his life.

Considering the fact that he'd fought terrorists in the Middle East and nearly become a POW himself, that meant a lot.

A corrupt cop was dangerous. Being in the custody

of a corrupt cop was even more dangerous. But he couldn't let Cassidy know about the concerns plaguing him. She already had enough worries of her own.

The door opened into this part of the station. A second later, Cassidy stepped inside. Just seeing her blonde hair and lithe figure made him instantly feel better. He rushed toward the bars separating them.

"Ty . . . how are you?" Her face pressed up against the barrier separating them. "Did they charge you?"

He nodded, recalling the events from last night. "They did. Apparently, they think they have enough evidence to make a case."

"They're drunk then." She shifted. "When's your arraignment?"

"Later today. The magistrate is only in town Mondays and Tuesdays, apparently. I'm fortunate that I don't have to wait until later in the week."

"Is Ricco handling things okay for you?" Her questions came out rapid fire.

"Yes, he's doing fine, Cassidy." He paused and studied her face. She looked different. Was that . . . his breath caught. "What happened to you, Cassidy?"

He reached forward and brushed the hair away. Sure enough, a huge knot was there. And a lot of makeup. She was covering up an injury of some sort.

She cringed and tried to step back, but Ty held her tight. She wasn't going to worm her way out of answering his question.

"It's nothing."

"Cassidy . . ." They'd been through too much for her to keep things from him.

Knowing Cassidy, she was probably trying to protect him. But the last thing Ty wanted was to be kept in the dark.

Cassidy sighed and glanced away, as if contemplating her options. Finally, her gaze met his again. The battered emotions in her eyes said it all. Something bad had happened.

"Someone attacked me last night."

A whoosh of air left his lungs. "What?"

Cassidy nodded, confirming that he'd heard correctly. "He was on the beach watching me. He started to run so I went after him—"

"Cassidy . . ." What had she been thinking?

"I let Mac know first. But it was too late. As soon as the man was out of sight, he circled around and was waiting for me. Hiding."

"What happened then?" Ty hardly wanted to know. Yet he *needed* to know. He wanted to claw out of this place and find the person who'd done this.

"He told me to back off, and then he slammed his gun into my head."

Anger boiled inside him. Ty should have been there to stop it. Yet he was powerless to help the woman he loved. That wasn't okay.

"Is that all that happened?" His voice cracked as he asked the question.

Cassidy cringed, and Ty knew there was more to the story.

After a moment of contemplation, she tugged down the collar of her shirt. "He did this."

Ty's eyes widened when he saw the cut there. The *cuts*. In the shape of an X. Over her heart.

His throat tightened until he could hardly breathe. "Oh, Cassidy."

"I'm okay." She grabbed his hand, her eyes pleading with him to believe her.

"He could have killed you." Ty couldn't even stomach that thought. What if he lost Cassidy, and all because he was being charged with the crime?

"He didn't."

"Not this time."

Cassidy frowned and stepped back, obviously not wanting to talk about this anymore. "I'm more worried about you."

He glanced at the door, making sure it was still closed and they had privacy. "Someone planted that gun in my house."

"I know. We're trying to figure out who. Me and Mac. The rest of the gang is behind you all the way. Anything they can do to help, they're willing to do."

"I appreciate that." He had a good group of friends, and for that he was grateful.

"Mac is even going up to Maryland now to talk to some of Cullum's associates. We'll find some answers."

"Like I said—I appreciate all of this. But I'm not sure how much good any of this is going to do. If there's someone on the inside, they're going to be able to manipulate information in any way possible."

"We're not going to let them do that," Cassidy said.

"I hope you're right. I hope you can stop them." But in his gut, Ty knew the odds weren't in his favor.

CHAPTER
TWELVE

CASSIDY AND TY had barely started talking when Quinton informed them their time was up.

She took one last glance at Ty. Saw his hunched muscles. Saw the concern stretched across his face like the reel of a tragic film. Saw the way it looked like an animal wanted to burst out of him and pounce on anyone that tried to mess with her.

She hated to leave him. But she had no choice at the moment.

Quinton waited to escort her. She gave a little wave to Ty and promised to see him later. Of course, she'd be showing up for his hearing, if they would let her get in. She wasn't sure how things worked around here.

Right now, she needed to remember that her assignment was Quinton.

She had to keep the main thing the main thing. Another piece of advice from Lucy's calendar.

She fell into step beside Quinton, waiting until they

left the cell block before saying, "He's not guilty, you know."

"We'll let the judge decide that. The murder weapon was found in his residence, as I'm sure you know. I know it must be hard for you to accept the fact that your boyfriend might be a killer."

He said the word "boyfriend" like the word left a bad taste in his mouth.

"If you need to talk, let me know," he continued. "I can explain the process."

Need to talk? It was so highly improper. But Cassidy pushed those feelings aside and remembered the end goal. "I would love to do that sometime. Professionally speaking, of course. That is what you meant, right?"

Surprise flashed across his face. "Yeah. Of course. I would never move in on someone else's woman. How about tonight?"

"That sounds good. The Docks?"

"I'll see you there. Six o'clock."

Her stomach roiled. Dinner with Quinton did not sound fun. No, she only wanted to be with Ty. But she'd do what she needed to find out who was behind this.

———

Five minutes later, Cassidy pulled to a stop in front of a bungalow tucked at the end of a long gravel driveway that seemed exceedingly secluded from the rest of the island.

The house itself was small and, unlike most of the

structures here on Lantern Beach, it wasn't on stilts to protect it from floodwaters. Bushes were overgrown along the edges of the building and, on either side of the small porch, were two stakes in the ground. Broken whelk shell after broken whelk shell was stacked on those stakes. The image reminded Cassidy of a Neanderthal who displayed skulls after a conquest.

Cassidy stared at the place and wondered if she should have brought backup with her.

Then again, if Serena—who'd not only worked for Cassidy but had also been a beat reporter—had come here alone, certainly Cassidy could handle it.

She approached the front door and pounded on the wood.

Silence answered her.

She glanced to the side and saw a beat-up sedan in an aluminum carport. A coat of pollen covered the burgundy paint, as if the vehicle hadn't been moved in a long time.

She'd bet anything someone was inside this place and not answering. Not moving, for that matter.

That wasn't going to work.

Cassidy pounded again, more urgently this time.

"I know you're in there!" she yelled. "It's about Elsa. It's important."

She waited. Silence ticked by. Was this visit an effort in futility? That's what it felt like.

Cassidy turned, about to leave, when the door opened.

Ernestine Sanders stood there.

Cassidy blinked when she saw the woman. She'd heard her name plenty of times, but she'd never actually seen the reclusive woman.

And she'd expected to see someone eccentric and colorful and . . . well, old.

But the woman standing in the entryway was probably in her late fifties or early sixties. Her salt-and-pepper hair was cut in a neat bob. A maxi skirt with a T-shirt graced her slender frame. Her face was surprisingly smooth and free of wrinkles.

"You must be Cassidy." The woman's eyes gleamed.

"Ernestine?" Cassidy needed to be sure. She knew this was the woman's house, but she shouldn't make too many assumptions.

"That's me."

Elsa had been in her seventies. And eccentric. And a colorful character around town.

Cassidy supposed she'd assumed Elsa's best friend would be similar.

Especially since she was reclusive.

"I'm sorry to show up unexpectedly," Cassidy said. "It was important."

"It sounded important." Ernestine hesitated, glancing behind Cassidy. "Would you like to come in for a minute?"

Cassidy nodded. "I would."

As Ernestine extended her hand back as a welcome, Cassidy stepped into the house. She studied her surroundings, still looking for signs that the woman was somehow unstable. But she saw nothing. Everything was clean and nicely decorated.

Newspaper copies were strewn across the dining room table, and that was the closest the place came to appearing junky.

"Deadline is tomorrow," Ernestine explained.

Yes, she was the editor of the newspaper, but she did everything from her home. In the summer Ernestine had Serena helping her. It seemed like an odd arrangement. But to each her own.

Cassidy shifted by the front door. "Are you covering the body found in the woods?"

Ernestine's eyes sparkled again. "Would you like to add a quote?"

"Not at all."

Ernestine clasped her hands in front of her. "I've enjoyed having you in town. You've made my job all the more pleasurable. How about some tea?"

This conversation was taking turns Cassidy hadn't planned on. "Sweet?"

"Is there any other kind?" Ernestine smiled, her eyes dancing with intelligence and amusement.

"I'd love some."

She disappeared into the kitchen and returned with the drinks on a weathered wooden tray. She set it on the coffee table and motioned for Cassidy to sit.

Cassidy lowered herself onto the dark blue cushion, praying she'd have the right words throughout this conversation. Ernestine and Elsa had been the best of friends. The last thing Cassidy wanted to do was stir up bad memories.

"You think Elsa was murdered, don't you?" Ernestine took a long sip of her tea, her eyes still on Cassidy.

Cassidy nearly spit out her drink. "What? Why would you ask that?"

Ernestine lowered her glass and held it daintily above her lap. "I've been waiting and waiting for someone to draw that conclusion."

Cassidy stared at Ernestine, unsure if she'd heard correctly. "You think Elsa was murdered?"

"Well, of course."

"Did you ever tell anyone?"

"I certainly couldn't tell the police."

"Why?"

"Because they're probably involved."

Cassidy set her drink down and leaned back, shock and surprise rippling through her. "Could you start at the beginning? Because this conversation is not going anything like I thought it would."

Ernestine also set her drink down and neatly folded her hands in her lap, the picture of demure.

"The night before Elsa died, she called me. She said she saw something suspicious at The Preserve. She was going to tell me more about it the next day after she finished her ice cream route. We never had that chance." Her voice faded with wistfulness.

Cassidy turned to fully face Ernestine. "Did she give you any hint as to what happened?"

"I started asking her questions. But before she could

answer, her ice cream truck suddenly started playing music. She said it did that the night before also but had never done it previously."

Cassidy sucked in a breath. The random music playing had started right before Elsa was killed. The thought wasn't comforting. Had the music actually gotten her killed—had it alerted the killer to her presence?

"So, you have no idea what happened?" Cassidy clarified.

"No solid clue. But I've been searching for answers the past year. Would you like to know what I discovered?"

CHAPTER
THIRTEEN

"I WAS SO pleased when someone bought Elsa's ice cream truck," Ernestine said, her shoulders relaxing a moment.

Cassidy held her breath. As much as she might have wanted to chat about her ice cream truck only a few days ago, it wasn't at the top of her priority list right now. Despite that, she waited patiently, realizing this could be a difficult subject for Ernestine.

"It's been quite an adventure," Cassidy said.

"Elsa just loved that job." A sad smile crossed her lips.

"How did the two of you become friends?" Again, it wasn't what Cassidy wanted to know. But maybe Ernestine needed to ease into this conversation. Cassidy was willing to do whatever it took—she just needed some answers.

"Elsa and I both moved here around the same time. We started going to book club together. We both loved mysteries. I hear you have an affection for them as well."

Cassidy's cheeks heated. How had Ernestine heard that?

"Serena told me," Ernestine explained, as if she could read the questions in Cassidy's gaze. "She was very impressed by your knowledge about police investigations."

"She exaggerated." *Downplay. Always downplay.* That was Cassidy's rule.

Ernestine raised her eyebrows. "I don't know about that. You know I used to be a reporter for the *Chicago Tribune*?"

Cassidy blinked. "I had no idea."

She nodded as if she enjoyed surprising people with that information. "Anyway, I kept the ice cream truck for several months. Elsa left her to me. I didn't know what to do with it. I certainly didn't want to sell ice cream myself. Within one week of putting it up for sale, I got the call that someone was interested in buying her."

"That would be me."

"Except you weren't the one who called." She stared at Cassidy, as if trying to read her thoughts.

Again, Cassidy felt herself shift uncomfortably. "That's true."

"I believe it was your father."

Cassidy nodded, relief loosening her lungs. She'd had a brain blip and couldn't remember what Samuel had told her. "That's right."

"Elsa would have been happy with how things worked out."

Cassidy took another sip of her tea, warming up to the conversation. "It sounds like Elsa was quite the character."

Ernestine smiled. "She was like the older sister I'd always wanted but never had. She was spunky and strange—but she embraced the strangeness."

Ernestine handed Cassidy a picture of herself with another woman. It had to be Elsa. Elsa with plastic-framed bright pink glasses. White hair that flipped out on the sides, as if its sassiness couldn't be contained. Elsa with a wide, mischievous grin and a silver necklace with an ice cream cone charm on the end.

"You ladies looked like two bugs in a rug."

Ernestine looked at the picture, sadness filling her eyes. "Elsa was all I had left. I didn't think I could go on without her. Life is always so much easier when you have a friend to walk side by side with you."

"I get that." It was another reason Cassidy was grateful for her time here on Lantern Beach.

"But then I had a new purpose—figuring out what happened to her."

"I thought you never left your house." Had Cassidy misunderstood?

"Well, I don't. But there's a lot I can do from right here. Lots of research." Ernestine shifted. "I know it probably seems strange to you that I don't go out. But the truth is, I don't know whom to trust. Staying home seems safer."

Agoraphobia, Cassidy realized. That was most likely what this boiled down to. Something must have sparked unrealistic fears about life outside the safe confinement of her home. Cassidy had met only one other person who suffered from the disorder.

"You said you discovered something?" Cassidy needed to get the subject back on track.

"That's right. Elsa considered herself a bit of a neighborhood watch or patrol."

Funny because that's what Mac had called Cassidy.

And it was what Cassidy felt like when she drove the ice cream truck. It gave her a great perspective on what was going on in the town and took her back to her days as a rookie cop.

"She noticed some strange meetings going on at night," Ernestine said. "She told me she was keeping an eye on things. I told her to be careful. I told her if people kept secrets, it was for a reason. And when people's secrets come out into the open . . . it's like fire hitting gasoline."

Cassidy's pulse spiked. She could understand the sentiment. Maybe she and Elsa were more alike than Cassidy had ever imagined.

"So, she called me. Told me she'd seen someone at The Preserve. Dressed as a police officer."

Cassidy swallowed hard. "Have you ever told anyone that, Ernestine?"

She scoffed "I couldn't. I certainly wasn't going to share it with the police. I'd have a target on my back."

"I see."

"Elsa had long suspected that something dirty was going on in this town." Her hand flew back as she said the word, nearly knocking a lamp down. Cassidy grabbed it, but, as she reached, her stitches pulled. She looked down at her shirt and saw blood leaking through.

"Oh . . . what happened?"

Cassidy pulled her collar down.

Ernestine's eyes widened. "Oh, my. An X? Something about that seems familiar . . ."

"What do you mean?"

"I feel like I've heard about it before."

Cassidy waited for her to remember where. But she couldn't.

Instead, she picked up the picture of Elsa again and looked at it.

Cassidy contemplated her next move. Finally, she pulled out Elsa's journal. "I thought you might want to see this . . ."

———

Ty glanced around the small courtroom as Wheezer escorted him inside.

Cassidy sat there, his friends beside her—Austin, Wes, Lisa, and Skye. He was thankful to have their support, but he hated for them to see him this way.

So much for setting a great example. For being a spiritual leader at Bible study.

Then again, Jesus had been persecuted for crimes He

hadn't committed. If this was the burden Ty had to carry, then so be it. He'd trust that God would somehow work this out for good.

Ty gave Cassidy a look, trying to convey to her that he was okay.

But then he saw the bruises on the side of her face. He remembered the cuts across her chest. And all of his assurances seemed to leave his mind.

If Cassidy wasn't careful, she was going to get herself killed.

He'd give anything just to be able to hold her. To watch the sunset together. To smell the sweet scent of her shampoo or feel her soft lips against his.

Cassidy didn't need to remind him how quickly this situation could spiral out of control. If the person responsible for this had the will and determination, he could not only frame Ty but also make sure Ty wasn't alive to deny the allegations.

The threat was real.

Ricco walked beside him as they took their place in the courtroom. The prosecuting attorney, who also happened to have a private practice on the island, presented his case to the magistrate, an elderly looking man with many wrinkles and what appeared to be a permanent frown. He listened silently, his eyes the only thing moving as his gaze swiveled back and forth from the prosecutor to Ty.

They covered the note with Ty's name on it, the fact people had seen him arguing with Cullum at the party, and the gun supposedly found at his house.

"We have one more piece of evidence, your honor," the prosecutor said.

More evidence? What were they talking about? Ty exchanged a look with Ricco.

"Upon examination of Mr. Chambers' truck, we found some keys beneath his seat," the prosecutor said. "These keys are confirmed to have belonged to Mr. McGrath."

Ty's pulse spiked. What?

"Someone planted those keys," he whispered to Ricco. "Cullum was never in my truck."

"Your honor." Ricco stood. "We were never notified about this evidence."

"We just got the official confirmation ten minutes ago that the keys were indeed Mr. McGrath's," the prosecutor said. "Even without the admission of the keys, we believe we have enough evidence to prove Mr. Chambers is responsible for this murder."

The magistrate frowned but said, "I'll allow it."

When it was his time, Ricco got up and defended Ty, arguing that the gun had been planted and that Ty had never seen it before, nor were his prints found on it. He also reminded the magistrate that the handwriting wasn't Ty's.

"Your honor, I'd like to remind you that this man is a decorated Navy SEAL," the prosecutor said, coming back at him. "He has the means and knowledge to escape from this area and never be found again."

"My client is an upstanding citizen who has put his

life on the line for this country," Ricco said. "That doesn't make him a risk. It makes him a hero."

The magistrate said nothing for a moment. He continued to sit there silently, as if considering the facts of the case.

"Bail is denied." The magistrate nodded toward Wheezer, indicating this was done, and they could leave.

Cassidy gasped behind him. He looked back in time to see her rush to her feet. Austin pulled her back down and shushed her.

Ty cast a look full of regret her way before Wheezer led him out of the courtroom.

Things were getting worse by the moment.

———

An unbearable ache formed in Cassidy's chest as she watched Ty being escorted from the courtroom.

"It's going to be okay," Austin whispered.

"Nothing is okay," Cassidy said. "I can't see anything good coming from this. Anything at all."

He squeezed her arm. "Keep the faith."

Lisa glanced over, a bleak disposition in her frown and a dullness in her eyes. "Let's all go to the Crazy Chefette to talk. Lunch is my treat."

Cassidy heard her but barely registered the words. She believed in the justice system. She'd left everything behind in order to pursue what she thought was right.

Now it felt like that very system was failing her

terribly. No, not failing *her*. Failing *Ty*.

Ricco circled back into the courtroom and pulled Cassidy aside. His quick motions conveyed his irritation.

"I'm sorry, Cassidy," he said. "That did not go as I thought it would. I've never seen a police department that operates like this one."

"Me neither." She crossed her arms, trying to ward off her heavy thoughts. "What next?"

"The county jail is full. I suppose that's good news—depending on how you look at it. That means Ty will have to stay here a while longer."

At least he'd be close. That was good since Cassidy couldn't leave the island.

"I'll keep doing everything I can to get him out. If you learn anything that can help his case, call me." Ricco handed her a business card. "I've already talked to Mac. I heard he's on his way up to Baltimore to talk to a few of Mr. McGrath's old friends. We're going to prove Ty is innocent, I promise."

Cassidy nodded. "Thank you."

She met with her friends again after Ricco walked away. They all looked at her with wide eyes, waiting for an update.

"How about if we go to my place?" Cassidy wasn't in the mood to deal with the public—the stares, the questions, the speculation. She knew how it worked. "There will be more privacy. Besides, I need to check on Kujo."

She was still in a daze when she climbed into her

sedan. Almost immediately, her phone rang. It was Mac. Based on a quick mental calculation, he was probably still three hours away from Maryland, if he hadn't hit traffic.

"How'd it go in court?" he asked.

Cassidy filled him in.

He grunted with disgust when she finished. "We're going to get to the bottom of this. Don't forget that."

"I'm trying not to." She was desperately trying to hold onto hope. It was becoming harder by the moment. "Did you find out anything?"

"Clemson just called. It appears our victim, Cullum McGrath, was indeed shot in the heart by the gun found at Ty's place."

Cassidy's heart thudded at the revelation. She'd been a fool to hope for anything differently. Yet, deep inside, she had.

She'd hoped to catch a break. To have something work in her favor. Yet that seemed impossible right now.

Still, she knew God was the God of the impossible. She needed to cling to His plan for this crisis—no matter how hard it might be to comprehend.

Cassidy cleared her throat. "Were any prints found on the gun?"

"Rumor is it was wiped clean."

"Of course." She should have guessed that.

"I was able to schedule a quick breakfast with Bozeman before I left," Mac continued. "Told him it was a tradition around here. He asked why he hadn't heard about it in the past three years, and I told him it was cause I'm getting forgetful."

Cassidy smiled at his schtick but only briefly. "Did you learn anything?"

"He's definitely hiding something," Mac said. "I was talking to him about the importance of balance and regrouping now that the summer season was over. Something changed in his gaze. He started talking about how hard it was to keep everyone happy."

"Is that really suspicious?" Cassidy asked. "I mean, that's true for all of us."

"The way he said it was with particular regret."

"Maybe he's having trouble at home. He is married, right?"

"He is," Mac said. "His wife is Vivian. No kids."

Cassidy leaned back in her seat, put down the window, and let the breeze roll over her. She'd seen Vivian once from a distance when they'd both been eating at Lisa's restaurant. But she'd never really spoken to the woman.

"What do you know about Vivian?" Cassidy asked.

"She seems nice enough. Kind of quiet, but she's a hard worker. Definitely his better half."

"What does she do here on the island? Does she work somewhere? Volunteer?"

"I think she works for a realtor during the summer months. In the off season, she's involved with Friends of the Library and does some other volunteering, I think."

Cassidy stored away that information, just in case it

came in handy.

"Clemson also said he was able to talk to Wheezer, but only briefly," Mac continued. "He just happened to stop by to pick up some documents at the clinic, so Clem struck up a conversation with him. Apparently, he's known the kid for a long time. Been treating his asthma since he was a preteen."

"Did Wheezer say anything interesting?" Cassidy asked.

"Interesting? Maybe not. But he did mention something about going out of town every opportunity he got."

"Is that because he's involved with something illegal?" Cassidy asked. "Like selling drugs maybe?"

"It could be. It's at least something to check out," Mac said. "How about you? Any progress with Quinton?"

She glanced at the clock on her dash. Two o'clock. She had plenty of time before her dinner with Quinton. "No, but I have a meeting with him tonight. He thinks it's more social than it actually is."

"Maybe you shouldn't meet with him one–on-one."

"We're meeting somewhere public. I'll be okay." As Cassidy said the words, her injuries from last night began throbbing.

Whoever was behind this wasn't playing games. He just might finish Cassidy at the first opportunity, especially when he discovered she was still investigating. But she wasn't giving up on this. No way. No chance. No how.

THE GANG CAME OVER and brought Cassidy something to eat. More like, Lisa tried to help comfort Cassidy with a sandwich consisting of peanut butter, sriracha, and a fried egg. For the side dish, she'd concocted a new take on macaroni and cheese—ramen and cheese. She'd even brought "dessert sushi," which consisted of rice crispy treats covered with a fruit roll up and stuffed with cream cheese and a brownie.

The woman was the queen of weird food combinations.

The group tried to cheer Cassidy up, but it was nearly impossible. She found comfort when they prayed for her. But she didn't have much of an appetite for Lisa's food.

The gang stayed for two hours before leaving. Cassidy promised to call if she needed anything.

In the silence after their departure, she mulled over

her thoughts, turning them over and over but going nowhere.

Someone knocked at the door. She drew her gun as she glanced toward it. Kujo began barking furiously.

No one was supposed to be here. And while she doubted the bad guy would be this obvious, she needed to be careful.

She heard something drop and saw a shadow move past the window.

Her muscles tightened again.

Slowly, carefully, she moved toward the door. She nudged the curtain out of the way but didn't see anyone. Kujo continued to bark.

"It's okay, boy," she whispered, rubbing his head.

With her gun still drawn, she pulled the door open and flung herself onto her deck.

No one was there.

But a package had been left on her welcome mat.

Glancing around one more time, Cassidy finally put her gun back into her waistband and leaned down.

There was no return address, but she remembered that Samuel had promised to send her something. This had to be it since she rarely got mail here.

She snatched the padded envelope from the deck, surveyed the area one more time, and then went inside, careful to secure all three locks on her door.

She didn't bother to sit down. No, she ripped the package open and sucked in a breath when she saw the jump drive inside.

After inserting it in her computer, she typed in the

encryption code Samuel had sent and waited with bated breath.

Finally, pages and pages of documents came up.

There should be answers here.

Would she be able to discover the real ringleader of DH-7? She didn't know. But this would be a start.

There were all kinds of documents here. Names. Numbers. Dates of crimes and of debts owed.

Toward the end were some memos.

Cassidy had never seen these before. She leaned back and studied each of them.

Someone—she assumed Raul—was sending threats to somebody about work they were doing for him. She glanced at the date. The memos dated back almost eight years.

Eight years ago? That was when the gang was first forming.

Why had these been saved? They had to be impor-tant. And why did they look so professional? DH-7 wasn't a gang full of former businessmen and women. They were street kids looking for a place to belong.

Cassidy's head swirled at the discovery.

She read the memos again. They were addressed to someone who went by the name Tango Mango.

Tango Mango?

She blinked.

This had to be a coincidence. It had to be.

Because Tango Mango was the pet name Lucy's father had given his daughter.

———

At six that evening, Cassidy met Quinton at an oceanside restaurant called The Docks. He wore his police uniform, but he seemed more laid-back than usual, like this was a casual meeting while he was off duty.

Without asking her what she wanted, he ordered some hot crab dip and a beer for himself. Cassidy ordered a water and some crab soup that she probably wouldn't eat. She made it clear she'd be paying for her own food, and Quinton didn't argue.

At least the weather was nice—so nice that Cassidy would love to be enjoying it with Ty.

The town's favorite local singer/songwriter Carter Denver sat in the corner crooning U2's "Walk On." He always added just the right soundtrack to Cassidy's day. If only she could walk on after all the trials she'd faced the last several months.

"So, have you always wanted to be an ice cream lady?" Quinton dug a piece of crispy French bread into the creamy crab dip.

Maybe this was her opening to ask more questions. She just needed to go with the flow. "No, but it's a pretty laid-back job."

"I'd say. Sounds nice. I could take a little less stress sometimes." He grinned while still chewing his food—it was quite the talent.

She purposefully brightened her eyes and leaned

toward him. "Did you know Elsa, the woman who owned the truck before me?"

He shrugged and tore off another piece of bread. "Not really. I'd just started working here a few months before those college kids found her dead."

"Must have been tragic."

"Everyone sure seemed to adore her around here. At least, she died doing what she loved. The music on the ice cream truck was still playing when I showed up even. "Ring Around the Rosy." It was kind of eerie, to be honest. And imagine those people's surprise when they went to buy ice cream and found her."

"It must have been terrible."

His eyes widened in a moment of sympathy before he continued eating. "Yeah, I'd imagine."

Cassidy took a sip of her own soup, hoping to seem companionable. "Were you the first one on the scene?"

"As a matter of fact, I was. I remember that day clearly."

She put her spoon down and played with a strand of her hair instead. "Why is that?"

"Because both the chief and Wheezer were having bad nights. The chief said he'd had a fight with his wife the night before, and Wheezer said he wasn't feeling well. Both were operating on empty, it seemed. That's why I was the one who responded to that call."

Cassidy stored those facts away. Or was the reason one of them looked terrible because they'd just killed someone?

Cassidy considered her words, considered the

consequences that asking her next question might cause. It was a risk she was going to take.

She shifted, playing with her straw and keeping her expression innocent. "I heard there were some strange things happening down at the lighthouse at night. You know anything about that?"

Quinton blinked, surprise registering on his face. "What do you mean by strange things?"

She leaned closer and lowered her voice. "Illegal things."

He shrugged, almost as if he was trying to rid himself of a heavy, itchy sweater. "There have always been illegal things happening on the coast. Have been for centuries, all the way back to the times of the pirates."

"What if some locals are involved?"

His cool gaze met hers. "We try to keep our streets clean. We patrol that area at night." He shrugged again, looking slightly annoyed—and it wasn't because of the seagulls circling above them. "But I thought we were meeting so you could ask questions about procedure and what happens next."

"We are. I was just making chitchat." Cassidy flashed a smile, trying to turn on the ditzy blonde persona Quinton seemed to respond to.

Instead, his eyes darkened. "Your boyfriend is probably going away for a long time. I'd start looking elsewhere."

"Look elsewhere for what?"

"A new boyfriend."

Cassidy forced her mouth to stay closed, to hold back her disgust at his words. A smart retort danced on the tip of her tongue.

Before Quinton could say anymore, his phone rang. He answered, muttered a few things, and quickly glanced up at Cassidy. He muttered some more, hung up, and stood.

"I have to run," he announced, dropping some cash on the table—enough to cover his portion.

Cassidy rushed to her feet, curiosity and concern clashing inside her. "What happened?"

"I'm sorry. I can't talk about it."

But the look he gave her scared Cassidy more than today's court hearing ruling had.

WHEN CASSIDY PULLED up at her place, she was surprised to see Chief Bozeman waiting in the driveway for her. He stood beside his police cruiser, leaning on it. His gaze looked hard as he watched Cassidy park.

Her defenses instantly went up. Had something happened to Ty? Was he here to deliver the bad news?

She rushed from her car but paused as her concern turned into cynicism. Something about Bozeman's look didn't imply that something tragic had happened. No, the gleam implied accusation.

"Chief. What's going on?" Did this have something to do with the phone call Quinton had gotten while Cassidy was with him? It was her best guess.

He crossed his arms, looking like a shark about to bite. "I heard you have some evidence for us."

"Excuse me?" What was Bozeman talking about?

Had something been planted at Cassidy's house? Her guard went up.

"You found a journal that used to belong to Elsa."

Her body tensed, but she tried not to show any reaction. Not until she had more information. She had only told a few people about it. None of them would have sold her out. "Why would you think that?"

Had Ty spilled the beans? She just couldn't see that happening. Mac? No. Clemson? She really didn't think so.

"Because Ernestine told us," he announced.

Cassidy sucked in a quick breath.

Ernestine? Why would she have done that? She'd said she didn't want to be a target.

But maybe if Cassidy had this journal, Ernestine wouldn't be a target. Cassidy would.

A surge of outrage rushed through her. How could Ernestine have given her up this easily? Even more— why had Cassidy trusted her?

Cassidy crossed her arms, knowing she needed to watch her words. "What did Ernestine tell you exactly?"

"That you found an old journal of Elsa's in the ice cream truck and that it might offer a clue about Elsa's death."

She pulled her purse closer. The journal was inside. Cassidy could deny it. But how would that help? Would Bozeman just get a search warrant? The police chief seemed to get whatever he wanted here in town.

Politics always seemed to be twisted—whether it

was a small town or a big city. People manipulated relationships and exploited the whole "I'll scratch your back if you scratch mine" philosophy. She couldn't stand it.

Cassidy raised her chin. "So, what if I did?"

Bozeman took a step closer. "Then I need to see it. I know that it implicates your boyfriend. I know he was dressed like a police officer that evening, and that Elsa said the killer was dressed that way. This is just one more piece of evidence against him."

Her spine stiffened. "You're wrong. This doesn't mean that Ty did this at all."

Challenge lit in his gaze. "Then who else would it be?"

Cassidy said nothing.

The chief chuckled and took a step back. He looked to the side, still laughing sardonically as if Cassidy had told a joke. "Are you implying that one of my men is behind this? You have a lot of nerve."

"I'm just saying you shouldn't be so quick to draw conclusions. You fixated on Ty from the start, and you haven't looked at any other possibilities."

Bozeman's cheeks reddened, and all humor disappeared. "I could arrest you for obstruction of justice."

Part of her didn't care. Let the man arrest her. But then Cassidy couldn't investigate. It would only further the chances that her identity would be discovered.

Nothing good would come from it.

"I want the journal, Ms. Livingston." He extended his nubby hand.

She waited, refusing to dive into her purse. Maybe it was just so she could aggravate the chief. Maybe she desperately wished another solution would hit her. The seconds ticked by.

"Ms. Livingston?" Bozeman's eyes narrowed again, and he sighed. "Don't think that I don't see what you're doing."

Cassidy's muscles tightened at his words. "What are you talking about?"

"You, Mac, and Clemson . . . you're all on the same side." Bitterness saturated his tone.

"We're on the side of the law."

He sneered. "So am I."

"No one said you weren't." Cassidy wasn't sure if he was a criminal—yet. She just knew he was incompetent. Other people in town were starting to see it also. Was that why Bozeman was buckling down so quickly with this case?

"No one needs to say anything." Bozeman scowled and held out his hand. "Now, I want the journal."

Finally, Cassidy grabbed the notebook. She'd taken pictures of the journal entries, so she could still study Elsa's words if she needed.

She hated that this made Ty look guilty. She somehow felt like she was failing him . . . again.

———

Cassidy slammed her keys on the kitchen table, ready to storm over to Ernestine's and give her a piece of her mind.

But she'd wait until morning.

Mostly because she didn't want to do anything to get herself arrested.

Thankfully, Mac called her again. Talking to him was just what she needed to calm down.

"Guess who I just met with?" Excitement tugged at his voice.

"Breena." Cassidy gave Kujo a nice long head rub before moving into the kitchen.

"You know it. And she was quite talkative. She said her gut has been telling her for a long time that Cullum was dead. I didn't tell her about the body—nothing definitive. Just that someone unknown had been found."

"Talkative can be a good thing in these cases." She poured herself a glass of water, trying to cool off.

"You better believe it. She recalled very clearly the last time she'd seen him."

Drink in hand, Cassidy dropped onto the couch, her body weary from everything that had happened. "Please tell me more."

"Let me start at the beginning," Mac said. "First of all, Cullum insisted on coming to Lantern Beach for vacation. Said he needed to mix some business with pleasure."

Just what kind of business was he talking about? It didn't matter. It was a good start. "Okay . . ."

"Cullum and Breena went down to the beach for that costume party that was going on. Cullum had too much to drink, apparently. And that was never a good thing. Breena accidentally spilled her beer on him, and he went ballistic. She said she thought he was going to kill her. That's when Ty stepped in. She credits him with saving her life."

That was no surprise. Ty was a hero in Cassidy's book every day.

"Cullum was mad about the intrusion, to say the least," Mac continued. "Cullum insisted he and Breena leave, so she did. She wasn't sure what was going to happen when they got back to the house they'd rented. But to her surprise, Cullum dropped her off. Said he had to meet with someone, and he took off on foot."

"On foot?"

"That's right. She said that was his preferred way to get around the island."

"Did she see Ty slip him a note?" Cassidy hardly wanted to ask the question, though she was confident of Ty's innocence.

"Of course not. There was no time for that."

"Did she say if she'd seen Ty before that costume party?" Cassidy tried to think through every possible angle the police might examine.

"She said they ate at the Crazy Chefette one night, and she had seen Ty across the restaurant. But they hadn't talked."

"So, she has no idea how Ty's information got into

his pocket?" Which was exactly what Cassidy had suspected.

"That's correct. Cullum did have some meetings set up while he was here. But he didn't give any indication he recognized Ty when they were in the restaurant earlier."

"How about his disappearance? Did she think anything of it?"

"Breena assumed he'd just been a jerk and took off, moving onto a better opportunity—or that he was running from the law. He was that type of guy."

"The police need to talk to her." Breena just had to stick with that story—that truth. Cassidy wouldn't put it past the person behind this to pay off Breena to lie. She took another long sip of water at the thought.

"I'm sure the police will once they have more evidence nailed down. But there were a couple of other things she said that I think you'll find interesting."

Cassidy sat up straighter, more anxious than ever to hear what he had to say. "What's that?"

"First, Cullum McGrath was deeply involved with the drug culture in Baltimore—and probably elsewhere. But I think we could have guessed that."

"A lot of criminals are." Drugs and crime went hand in hand.

"But he was also a bookie," Mac said.

"A bookie?" Cassidy repeated, surprise coursing through her.

"That's right. He loaned people money, and things got ugly when they didn't pay him back. She thinks that was one of the reasons he was on the island. The other thing is that he kept talking about meeting with someone named Shorty."

Shorty? Cassidy hadn't heard about anyone in this area with that nickname. Then again, he could have been a tourist or even just someone who'd come to town for this "business."

"Was that the night he disappeared?" She knew the chances of tracking this person down were slim.

"No, the night before."

"It's worth looking into."

"One more thing: I asked her about those business cards," Mac said. "And she said Cullum never kept the contents of his wallet in a plastic bag—not even at the beach."

That made sense.

Cassidy knew just the person she needed to talk to.

Jimmy James.

If there was trouble in town, he always seemed to know about it.

———

It only took a couple of phone calls for Cassidy to find out where Jimmy James was staying now. Apparently, his roommate had bailed on him a few weeks ago, so he'd moved into a small truck camper at a local RV resort.

However, when Cassidy pulled up to his new place, no one answered his door. She took a step back and looked at the place. The camper was probably thirty years old, with green stuff growing on the sides. Too much litter had gathered in the landscaping crevices for it to look in any way welcoming. Cassidy could only imagine what the inside looked like.

She glanced behind her at the other RVs. There were all types here—nice ones, well-kept ones, and junky ones like the one belonging to Jimmy James.

Where could he be now? There was no telling. Probably up to something no good.

It was growing dark outside, and the town was beginning to settle down. But Cassidy wasn't ready to do that. She had too much on her mind—too much at stake. As long as she had a smidgen of energy, she needed to use it to find the real killer.

On a whim, Cassidy drove to the lighthouse and parked in the shadows there, cutting the lights. She'd brought Kujo, who panted happily in the seat beside her.

Cassidy shuddered as she looked at the lighthouse, remembering the last time she'd been here. She'd almost died. That day had ended a chapter of her life and started a new beginning.

Yet the book of her life was so far from being done.

There was still the trial for DH-7. Then there was the strange information she'd just discovered about Lucy. Why was her nickname used on one of the memos from DH-7? Could it be a coincidence? Possibly.

Cassidy wouldn't rest until she knew for sure. The pieces of her life may be more connected than she'd ever thought. The realization was chilling, to say the least.

A man who chases two rabbits catches neither.

Day-at-a-Glance advice. But wasn't that what Cassidy was doing now?

Before she dug too deeply into that mystery, she needed to solve this one first.

From the safety of her car, she watched the seashore in the distance. The midget-like trees around her swayed with the breeze. The moon offered just enough light to illuminate the waves—and they were a sight to see. Probably five lines of breakers rolled, crashing one after the other.

The ocean was a formidable foe—beautiful but deadly. She'd seen enough beachfront rescues this summer to know that.

The sand stretching along the shore appeared empty —no one was in sight.

Not yet. But maybe soon.

This was the spot she and Ty had seen some suspicious activities going on. If Cassidy could figure out who the officer was who was involved in the criminal happenings here, maybe she'd have some answers to help solve Ty's case as well.

It was a long shot, but she had to do something. Sitting alone at her cottage couldn't be the solution.

She waited there for three hours. Three long hours. She ate two beef jerky sticks—well, actually just one since she gave the other to Kujo.

But nothing happened. No one showed up.

"I think all of this was in vain, buddy." She rubbed the dog's head.

He panted and leaned into her, wanting more attention.

Finally, she drove back to her cottage. Maybe a good night's rest would help her.

Tomorrow, Cassidy would go to see Ty again. She'd go talk to Ernestine. And she'd find some answers.

Back at her place, she locked her doors behind her, patted Kujo on the head, and went to take a shower. After she towel-dried her hair and put her pajamas on, she stepped into her bedroom.

As soon as she did, she froze.

What felt different in here?

Her muscles clenched as she surveyed the dark space. And where was Kujo? He usually waited outside the bathroom door for her.

Before Cassidy could figure it out, she heard a footfall behind her.

CASSIDY HIT the floor as someone collided with her. She flipped onto her back, ready to fight.

The masked man had returned. And he held a knife.

Her blood pressure surged.

As the man lunged at her, Cassidy turned, rolling toward the door.

She reached for something—anything—that she could use to protect herself. There was nothing. She'd left her gun on her nightstand, well out of reach.

The man came at her again.

She rolled again. This time, she hit her bed.

She had nowhere else to go in the small room.

The man let out a grunting chuckle, like he knew he had her trapped.

And delighted in it.

That was unacceptable.

Cassidy kicked her legs in the air, and the knife flew

from his hands. As he lunged for it, she raised her knee and caught him in the gut.

A moan escaped him.

He forgot about his knife and turned to Cassidy. He reached for her neck, squeezing it, cutting off her oxygen.

Cassidy clawed against his grip, desperate for air.

It was not going to end this way. It couldn't.

"I told you to leave this alone," the man whispered. "Why can't you let things go?"

If he expected her to answer, he was mistaken. Stars formed in the periphery of her vision. Cassidy wasn't going to last much longer.

She desperately tried to pry his fingers from her windpipe.

There had to be something she could do to end this before this man ended her.

She reached behind her. Her fingers felt something. Was that . . . a cord?

Her night stand should be there. This had to be the cord for her lamp.

She tugged on the cord—then jerked it hard. The heavy glass base of the lamp hit the man's head then crashed to the floor and shattered.

The distraction gave Cassidy enough time to crawl away, climb to her feet, and . . . run.

She knew she didn't have time to grab her gun. The best thing she could do right now was to get as far away from the man as possible. Because if he caught her again, he'd kill her.

Pain jolted through her foot.

She must have stepped on some glass as she fled.

She cringed at each jab of pain.

She wouldn't get far with this agony.

Instead, she ran over to Ty's place and ducked behind his truck.

She tried to control her breathing as she watched and waited. She didn't have much time, just enough to gather herself.

The man stomped down the stairs, slowly, carefully. His head swiveled, scanning around him as he searched for Cassidy.

As he passed Elsa, an animal-like sound came from inside.

Animal like? Kujo. The man must have locked the dog in her truck while Cassidy was in the shower.

Now the canine was snarling and barking . . . but unable to get out.

Cassidy held her breath as she watched and waited for the man's next move.

"I know you're out here," the man yelled amidst Kujo's angry snarls. "Why don't we just make this easy?"

No way.

Cassidy crouched lower.

Who was behind that mask?

Cassidy glanced down and caught the reflection of something on the ground. A wrench. From when Ty had been fixing her truck. He must have dropped it.

She picked the heavy tool up and wrapped her fingers around the center.

The man started toward Ty's place, and she prepared herself for battle.

As he rounded the truck, Cassidy charged toward him. As soon as the man was close enough, she slammed the wrench against his temple.

The next instant, the man was on the ground and out cold.

———

Cassidy didn't waste any time. She found some zip ties in Ty's shed—he always kept some handy—and rushed back to the man. She bound his arms and feet together. For good measure, she used two more zip ties to connect the binds around his hands and feet, essentially hogtying him.

That should keep him in one place long enough for her to get some help. But first she wanted to find out who this man was.

Cassidy reached forward, shoved down a strange touch of anxiety, and jerked his mask off.

She blinked at the face she saw.

He was . . . totally unfamiliar. The redhead had a heavy jawline, pockmarks mixed with a few stray freckles, and small ears that stuck out, making them appear larger.

He moaned and blinked. Yeah, he'd have a headache. And Cassidy didn't feel sorry for him.

"Who are you?" she growled, squatting in front of him. As she did, the cuts on her chest ached, reminding her of what this man had done to her.

The man scowled while simultaneously flinching. "Noneya."

Cassidy somehow had to get her phone and call . . . call who? The police? That didn't seem like a great move considering one of them had probably hired this guy.

But she couldn't keep him here either, nor did she want to let him go.

She'd cross that bridge in a moment.

"Who paid you to come here?" Cassidy shoved him on his back using her uninjured foot.

"Who said someone paid me?" He smirked.

"Glad to see you still have your humor." She narrowed her eyes, hating it when people took her for a fool. "I know someone gave you some money to do their dirty work."

"Maybe I just don't like you."

"If you simply 'just don't like me,' why would you tell me to back off? You've got an agenda."

Kujo barked in the background, clawing at the window of the ice cream truck. A balmy breeze seemed to try and calm everyone down, but it didn't work. Cassidy wasn't in the mood to play any games.

The man snapped his mouth closed and scowled. "You're not getting anything out of me. I should have finished you while I had the chance."

"Tell me who's behind this, and maybe I'll make it easier on you."

He grunt-chuckled again. "I doubt that."

"Fine, then spend the next several months behind bars. Because I will be pressing charges." She took a step away. "Maybe Kujo can get some answers from you. He is trained to attack on command."

His eyes widened. "Wait. What?"

Cassidy paused halfway to Kujo, but only for a moment. "You heard me."

"You don't scare me. And I've got nothing to say. You'll have to kill me first!"

She walked to her driveway, opened Elsa's door, and let Kujo out. The dog ran over to her attacker and began barking and growling.

The man screamed and began trying to scoot away.

"I'm going to leave Kujo here to guard you while I go get my phone." She turned toward Kujo. "Kujo, guard."

She said it like it was a command they'd practiced before. It wasn't. But she hoped the man didn't know that.

The man tried to squirm away, but with his hands and feet all tied together, it was nearly impossible. His pale face and frantic motions were enough to satisfy Cassidy.

Good. That was exactly what Cassidy wanted.

She limped upstairs and grabbed her cell phone.

———

Cassidy carefully watched Quinton's expression as he observed the man she'd apprehended. The officer didn't show any signs of recognition, but the jury was still out as to who had hired her attacker. She'd reserve her judgment.

Cassidy called off Kujo, who now happily gnawed a bone in her driveway, while Cassidy finished taking care of this catastrophe. She'd even snapped some photos of the man with her phone, just for future reference. *Document, document, document.*

She'd told Quinton what had happened, and he'd taken notes.

Quinton's gaze flickered back to the man squirming on the driveway. "You certainly did a good job of tying him up."

"I was a Girl Scout."

"They teach you that in scouting?"

"I got a special badge for taking down men who act like pigs."

He grunted and stared at her, as if trying to ascertain if she was joking or not. "Tell me again what happened. I just need to hear it one more time."

Cassidy went through the story again. When she finished, Quinton shook his head. He looked genuinely surprised, but he could be a good actor. "And you have no idea why someone would do this?"

"I'd imagine the person who set up Ty is behind this."

It almost looked like Quinton rolled his eyes. "You really think someone is setting up your boyfriend?"

"I know they are."

"And who would do that?" Quinton's eyes glinted in the darkness.

She crossed her arms and kept her gaze steady. "The person who killed Cullum McGrath, of course."

"They would have had to plan it several months in advance."

"I know that."

"You think you could untie me?" The man on the ground pulled against his restraints, to no avail.

"We're not talking to you right now, but you'll get your turn soon enough," Quinton snapped before turning back to Cassidy. "I don't think you should get your hopes up. My suspicions are that your boyfriend will be going away for a long time."

Anger burned inside her. Quinton was awfully presumptuous and arrogant—two qualities she couldn't stand. "Not if I have anything to do with it."

"I highly doubt an ice cream woman is going to be able to help in a case like that."

He'd certainly changed his tune from earlier when he'd seemed eager to impress her. What had happened? It didn't matter. Not now.

"Don't underestimate me," Cassidy said, her voice low and steady.

"Just don't get your hopes up. I'll take this guy in and press charges. I've got your official statement. But after that stunt you pulled with the journal, you're on the chief's bad side."

"Is that why you were called away from dinner earlier?"

He shrugged. "Maybe. Until we figure out what's going on here, I'd be careful. Maybe you even want to get out of town for a while."

Cassidy's gut twisted. She couldn't leave this place. And, if she did, it wouldn't be without Ty. "Thanks for the tip, but I'll stick around."

"Have it your way. But remember what I said. Be careful."

CADY HEARD the gathering in the room behind her —the laughter, the jovial talking, the loud music. It had morphed from a meeting, to more people joining them, to an all-out party. She dared not come out from beneath the desk.

But she desperately wanted to know what was happening.

After ten minutes, an internal pressure built up inside her so much that she couldn't take it anymore.

Remaining beneath the desk, she reached her arm out and felt around until her hand connected with the computer.

She was going to finish what she started.

Carefully, she peeked out for just long enough to insert the jump drive and hit a few keys. She quickly studied the screen, looking for confirmation that everything was working as it should.

She released her breath.

Everything was being saved, just as it was supposed to happen.

Cady slid back under the desk to wait until the task was complete.

Her thoughts drifted again. If she were to die tonight here in Raul's office, who would mourn her?

She wasn't sure where all the melancholy thoughts were coming from. But they were there. And, as much as Cady might like to ignore them, they were too pressing. They stole her attention and pushed to the forefront of her mind.

Her parents would mourn her, of course. But then they'd resume life. She was never a part of their schedule or routine, and they would keep busy with work and social activities. Cady would simply become a part of their story, and people's sympathy toward them would only heighten their influence.

Ryan would miss her. Right? Of course.

Why was Cady even asking that question?

Yet she didn't feel a definite yes in her heart. That couldn't be a good sign.

Her colleagues at the police department would attend her funeral. Say what a great cop she was. How they liked it when she brought in donuts for them on Fridays.

But none of that was what she wanted for her life. Not deep down inside.

Cady really wanted stability. She wanted a core group of people who truly loved her. Who shared their lives with her.

That was something she didn't have.

When Cady finished with this assignment, she was going to make some changes. If anything, this mission had opened her eyes. Made her re-evaluate her life. Given her a good reality check.

She didn't want to be like her dad. Yet that was exactly who she was becoming. Someone whose work consumed them. Defined them. Took first priority in life.

But what would it take to change?

She poked her head out again. A graph on the computer showed the download was almost done.

Cady hoped desperately this contained the information she needed.

She was so tired of this assignment. Tired of sleeping on a dirty bed in this old apartment complex. Tired of pretending. Of putting her life on hold.

Finally, the computer dinged.

It was ready.

Cady released her breath and grabbed the jump drive from the computer. She slid it into her pocket and closed the files, leaving the computer as she found it.

Now she had to figure out how to get out of here.

CHAPTER
EIGHTEEN

TODAY'S GOALS: FIND THE
PERSON WHO REALLY KILLED
CULLUM MCGRATH. CALL
SAMUEL. STAY OUT OF TROUBLE.

CASSIDY HADN'T GOTTEN any sleep last night, not after everything that had happened.

The first thing she'd done after Quinton left with her attacker was to study the area where the man had gotten inside. He'd somehow jimmied one of the windows, breaking the latch and slipping inside.

She should have been more careful—and she would be in the future.

Cassidy had also been left with the realization that someone had hired this man. He wouldn't tell her who that person was, but Cassidy had a narrow pool of suspects—namely Bozeman, Quinton, or Wheezer.

As the sun peeked over the horizon, she sat at the computer with a strong cup of coffee and did a reverse image search for the man who'd invaded her home last night.

It didn't take long for her to get results.

The man's name was Ed Kyle, and he had a criminal

record. He'd been charged with assault and battery, driving under the influence, possession of drugs . . . the list went on and on.

He'd been released from jail in Delaware three months ago.

His mug shot showed someone who looked even scarier than the face she'd seen last night. In his police photo, his eyes were dark and empty. She recognized the look because she'd seen it plenty of times while working as a cop.

They were the hardened eyes of a true criminal, someone who was immersed in the life full-time.

He'd obviously been hired to scare her off. Maybe to plant the evidence framing Ty.

But by whom?

Cassidy continued with her search and saw that he was from . . . Greenville, North Carolina.

Wasn't that where Quinton said he was from?

Could this be her first real lead?

Possibly. Yet Quinton hadn't seemed to recognize the man. He had been called away from their dinner at The Docks. He said it was because of the journal, but what if it was to orchestrate last night's attack?

She glanced at her watch.

It was time to get to the police station and visit Ty. Her stomach clenched when she realized that Ed Kyle would probably be there also, locked in the cell next to Ty. At the thought of it, the cuts on her chest panged.

Cassidy would like to give the man a piece of her mind . . . plus some. She'd need to keep herself in check.

What kind of story was the Lantern Beach PD going to try to feed her about the man? She had no idea.

But she couldn't wait to see Ty. She longed for the day he could hold her in his arms again. Until then, she'd keep fighting for him for as long as it took.

———

Ty blanched when Cassidy appeared through the door leading to his cell. He'd been looking forward to seeing her, but now that she came into focus . . . his worry ricocheted. On the outside, she looked good. Great actually. Her jean shorts, the blousy white top, and sandals were a nice look on her.

But it was the aura about her that concerned him. She smiled, but the action didn't reach her eyes. No, heaviness seemed to permeate each of her movements.

"Cassidy . . ." He leaned into the bars, his heart physically aching that he couldn't comfort her.

She glanced around before pausing in front of him. "How are you?"

"How am I? I'm the least of my worries right now. What happened? Did that guy come back?" Anger surged up his spine at the thought.

She didn't say anything for a moment, which was answer enough.

"Cassidy . . ." he pleaded.

She pushed a long, wavy hair behind her ear—hair he loved to feel against his cheek. Hair that smelled like berries and the seashore. Something was obviously wrong, based on her shifting gaze.

"Someone was waiting in my house last night." Cassidy's face looked stoic, as if she tried to hide away any emotions.

"What did he do to you?" The words came out with a seething hiss. This had to end. It wasn't okay. None of it.

"Nothing I couldn't handle."

Ty gripped the bars, anger coursing through him. "Cassidy . . ."

"I'll be fine."

"No, you're not fine. He could have killed you. I should be out there, protecting you."

"I'm a detective," she whispered. "I can defend myself."

"Everyone needs someone to have their back."

She opened her mouth, as if to argue, but then stopped. "You're right. But none of this is your fault. It's mine. I shouldn't have pushed you to go searching in The Preserve. If I hadn't, none of this would have happened."

"Cassidy . . . you can't blame yourself. You had no idea what that journal would set in motion."

"I should have listened to you."

He squeezed her hand. "Please, don't. Don't beat yourself up. I don't blame you for this."

"I appreciate that." But her eyes didn't look convinced. "You and I both know the truth."

"Cassidy . . ." How was he ever going to reach her?

Ty tried to find the words, but there was nothing else he could say to convince her.

Finally, Cassidy glanced around, and a new emotion entered her gaze. "You're in here alone again? Why is no one else in here with you?"

Ty shrugged, wondering why she was asking. "There were some guys in here last night, but they were released."

"Did one of them have red hair?"

"No, they both had brown hair. Why?" Then he realized the truth. "The man who attacked you . . ."

He was arrested, yet . . . "He's not here."

Cassidy swallowed so hard her throat looked visibly strained.

"Where else would he be?" Ty did not like the sound of this. At all.

"I'll definitely be asking as soon as I leave here." Cassidy paused. "Ernestine told the police about the journal. They're going to use that as more evidence in the case against you."

Great. More evidence. This hadn't even been planted. Yet how could he disprove any of it? He couldn't.

"Did Ricco tell you if the police sent that note out for a handwriting analysis?" Cassidy asked.

"He said they did, but that these things take a long time to hear back on."

"Yeah, they usually do. I guess I was just hoping . . ."

"It's going to be okay, Cassidy. Whatever happens."

Her expression shifted from worried and frantic to dull. "I wish I had your faith, Ty."

"I've had a lot of practice putting it into action." Ty watched as Cassidy lowered her head until her forehead touched the bars. He reached toward her and stroked her hair, relishing the feel of the silky strands across his fingers. "I love you, Cassidy. I'm sorry you're going through all of this."

"There you go. Thinking about me when you're the one behind bars."

"Those guys I told you about—the ones who were here last night? I overheard them talking."

Cassidy's eyes brightened with curiosity. "Okay . . ."

Ty released a long breath. Cassidy was smart and competent. She'd use the information wisely. He had to trust her.

Still, he hesitated a moment before sharing, "They said that those deals that go down at the Point . . . they happen on Wednesdays."

"They told you that?"

"No, they were talking loudly while I was trying to sleep."

"You think this is the same meeting that we saw that cop at?"

"Yeah, I do."

"I'll see what I can find out."

His throat burned. "Be careful, Cassidy. I don't like any of this."

WHEN CASSIDY LEFT TY, her heart felt heavy and burdened. Ty looked like a caged tiger behind those bars. More than anything, she wanted to help him. She wanted to feel his arms around her. She wanted to be with him . . . forever.

The thought nearly felt startling. Yet it wasn't. Hadn't she known that for a long time? Yet she and Ty hadn't talked about forever. No, she'd made Ty promise to only take this day by day.

Wasn't that all she could promise? She had no idea what the future held for her—jobwise or even personally. Would she ever be safe anywhere? Would the people she loved ever not be a target because of her?

She fisted her hands at her sides as the thoughts warred inside her.

She couldn't waste any more time. She needed to check in with someone to see what had happened to Ed Kyle. Hopefully Quinton had simply taken the man somewhere else. But would the officers here really think that much ahead? Would they really show that much concern for Ty?

It seemed unlikely.

Before heading out, Cassidy headed to Wheezer's office to ask him a question. As his voice sounded on the other side of the door, she paused and waited.

"I'm doing what I can," Wheezer muttered.

A couple of seconds passed, like the person he was talking to was responding. He must be on the phone.

"I know. Listen, it's all going to work out. Nothing's going to get in our way."

Nothing's going to get in our way? What did that mean?

Wheezer had been at the bottom of Cassidy's suspect list, but maybe that was a mistake.

He definitely had the opportunity. He'd been at the party that night and had seen Ty. He could have planted evidence at Ty's place when he went there with the search warrant. And now, according to Clemson, he was going out of town every chance he got. What exactly was he doing when he left town? Something illegal?

No, more likely it had to do with this side business he had going on. Drugs? Maybe he felt like he was going nowhere here in Lantern Beach. Maybe Cullum had given him the opportunity to escape this life and then snatched it back.

Cassidy didn't have enough information to know— or even feel confident in any of her theories.

"I should know something soon," Wheezer continued. "Maybe tonight. I'll let you know as soon as it's done."

When Cassidy heard the phone hit the cradle, she stepped into the doorway. Wheezer glanced up in surprise. "Ms. Livingston. Hi."

"Everything okay?" She glanced at the phone. "I couldn't help but overhear part of the conversation."

His cheeks reddened. "Everything's fine."

Cassidy didn't say anything, only looked at him and waited.

He let out a sigh and raked a hand through his hair. His pensive expression made it clear he was contemplating how much to tell her.

Cassidy continued to wait, hoping the silence would be enough pressure for him to spill everything.

As his gaze hit hers again, Cassidy knew she'd hit the jackpot.

"Look, I've been applying for other jobs," he blurted. "I don't want anyone to know."

Other jobs? She recalled the conversation she'd overheard and realized he might be telling the truth. "That's why you've been going out of town?"

He nodded and pulled out his inhaler, taking a quick puff. "Yeah, I don't know how you know I've been going out of town, but I'm ready to be finished with this place."

Cassidy crossed her arms, not ready to clear him yet. "Why's that?"

Wheezer glanced around again. "I don't know. It's . . . it's just time."

She stepped into the office and closed the door, hoping he might be more open if they had privacy. "Are you not happy with things here?"

Wheezer swallowed hard and remained on the other side of the desk, almost like he needed the furniture to separate him from Cassidy. For a cop, the man could be easily intimidated.

"You can tell me," Cassidy prodded. "I would want to leave if I worked here."

"Why would you say that?"

"Because there's something not right with this police department. You're smart enough to see it too, aren't you?" Flattery was a great tool for making people open up.

Cassidy was keenly aware that she was taking a risk here. She could blow her cover if she wasn't careful. But this was her opportunity to talk to Wheezer and get information. She could see in his eyes that he wanted to chat, and Cassidy needed to push this as far as she could.

"I don't know." He shrugged uncertainly.

"Sure, you do."

He leaned against his desk, a fine sheen of sweat across his forehead. He took another puff of his inhaler. Glanced around again. "Look, I don't want trouble. I just want to find another job and move on. End of story."

"Clemson said you're a good guy. Good guys don't turn a blind eye to bad things happening around them."

He tugged at the collar of his dark blue uniform. "It's . . . it's not that simple."

"You think Ty was set up, don't you?"

He tugged his collar again. "I've always liked Ty. He helped my mom when her car broke down and she didn't have money to fix it. He worked on it free of charge."

That sounded like Ty. "So what's going on?"

"I can't talk to you about these things. It will only cause trouble."

"I'll forget this conversation ever happened."

"There are things that don't add up."

"Like?" Cassidy felt like she was so close to getting some answers. So close. She needed him to keep going.

Wheezer lowered his voice. "Ty's a smart guy. He wouldn't leave the murder weapon in his house. And he loves his truck. He would have cleaned it out since October and found those keys, if they had really been there that long."

Her heart spiked with excitement. "So you do think he was set up?"

He rubbed his jaw. "I do. But I can't bring it up. Because I know that either Bozeman or Quinton are probably behind it."

At least someone else was seeing things Cassidy's way. It brought her a strange measure of relief. She'd never win this on her word alone. "What are we going to do about it?"

"I'm doing what I can. I'm trying to watch out for Ty and to gather any other evidence I can. I don't have a lot of pull around here, though."

"Don't underestimate yourself." She mentally switched gears. "By the way, where's the man who attacked me last night?"

His eyes widened, and he drew his head back. "You didn't hear?"

"Hear what?" She already didn't like where this was going.

"Quinton was supposed to tell you."

"Tell me what?"

"Ed Kyle escaped custody. We haven't been able to locate him."

Adrenaline pumped through Cassidy's body as she climbed into her car after talking to Wheezer. Eventually, she'd need to talk to either Quinton or Bozeman and find out why she wasn't informed that the man who tried to kill her had escaped. Apparently, Quinton was out searching for the escapee, and she wasn't sure where Bozeman was.

It was another case of the police department being incompetent. She shouldn't be surprised, yet they always managed to go above and beyond when it came to disappointing her.

Until she was able to talk to Quinton and figure out

what had happened last night, there was something else she needed to do.

She needed to talk to Ernestine. She had some serious questions to ask her.

Cassidy drove to Ernestine's house, trying not to get worked up. It was too late. Between Ed's escape, Ty's imprisonment, and her throbbing injuries, she was fired up and her emotions desperately wanted to boil to the surface.

At the house, Cassidy slammed her car door and charged up to Ernestine's porch.

Cool head, Cassidy. Cool head.

She pounded on the cheerful yellow door and waited.

Nothing.

Okay, this was getting old. Cassidy knew Ernestine didn't leave her home. That meant, she was most likely just avoiding Cassidy.

Nice try, but that wasn't going to work.

She knocked again. Waited some more.

Nothing.

With a heavy sigh, Cassidy moved to the window and peered inside.

Nothing caught her eye.

Feeling more irritated by the minute, she hurried to the back side of the house. Maybe—just maybe—Ernestine had gone into the backyard. Cassidy highly doubted it, but she'd double-check before drawing any conclusions.

But the backyard was empty.

Cassidy crept up the weathered, cracked wooden steps to the back door. She knocked on the glass pane atop the door. She knew it was probably futile, but she tried anyway.

It was no surprise when Ernestine didn't answer. Again.

"Come on, Ernestine." Cassidy tapped her foot impatiently. "You can't hide. Own up to what you did."

With one last effort, she cupped her hands around her eyes and peered inside one more time.

She sucked in a deep breath.

Ernestine lay on the floor. And Cassidy was pretty sure she wasn't breathing.

AN HOUR LATER, Cassidy waited on the periphery of the scene. She lingered in the corner of Ernestine's immaculately clean kitchen, giving first responders the chance to do their job.

After finding the woman, Cassidy had checked for a pulse—which was still steady and strong—and called 911. Wheezer had come. Clemson had come. An ambulance had come.

And now Ernestine was laid out on the couch with an oxygen mask on her face and another paramedic carefully monitoring her.

Cassidy had soaked in the scene as she waited for help to arrive. There was no blood, nor was there any sign of struggle here in the house.

Had Ernestine had a heart attack? Passed out because of low blood sugar?

Cassidy didn't have a great feel for what had happened to the woman, but to say she was concerned would be an understatement. She'd revealed information about a cop, and she'd almost died.

Whoever was behind this was ruthless and would do anything to get away with his crime.

At the moment, Clemson glanced at Cassidy. He knelt beside Ernestine, speaking in soft tones while also instructing the paramedics. After a few minutes, he stood, patted Ernestine's hand, and then made his way over to Cassidy.

"She's going to be okay," he said.

Cassidy pulled her arms tighter around her chest, anxious to hear his take on Ernestine's condition. "What happened?"

"It looks like she either fainted or fell and hit her head." He shoved his hands into the pockets of his bright blue shorts. He'd obviously been off duty when called in.

"Just like Elsa?" Cynicism stained Cassidy's words.

Clemson's lips pulled into a grim line. He'd appeared to have already thought about that. He gave a curt nod. "Just like Elsa."

Cassidy glanced around to make sure no one else was listening before whispering, "Clemson, she was afraid of being a target if she admitted her suspicions about a dirty cop to anyone. Well, yesterday she called the cops and told them about the journal I'd found. The next thing we know, I find her, and she's almost dead."

Saying it out loud only made Cassidy feel more uneasy and drove home the fact that she and Ty could also fall victim here if they weren't careful.

"I don't like this." Clemson studied her face, fatherly concern in his gaze. "Especially after what's happened to you. You think your attacker started at your place and then came over here?"

She swallowed hard as she pictured it playing out. "It's a good possibility. He got out of police custody. I can't believe they haven't made more people aware that we have an escaped prisoner, an attempted killer."

Clemson pressed his lips together and closed his eyes. "This is getting more dangerous by the moment."

"I agree." She glanced back at Ernestine. The woman was coming to but still looked groggy. "What now? Are you taking her to the clinic?"

"I'm afraid it might affect her heart if she wakes up there."

Cassidy tilted her head, uncertain of what he was getting at. "What do you mean?"

He let out a long sigh, almost as if his thoughts were burdensome. "Ernestine and I go way back. She was friends with my late wife. Ernestine told me I was allowed to fill you in on her condition. Said it was the least she could do since you saved her."

"Okay."

"Not only is she agoraphobic, but she also has a heart condition. I'm not sure the benefits of taking her to the clinic would outweigh the risks."

"What happened to make her this way, Doc Clem? She told me she used to be a reporter up in Chicago. Most people don't walk away from that to start their own newspaper on an island."

"There was a break-in at her home," he explained. "She walked in on the middle of it, and the two men left her for dead. She apparently was never the same after that."

Cassidy could imagine how traumatic that might be.

"So, you're going to leave her here at her house?" The woman didn't appear to have anyone now that Elsa was gone. It was a sad commentary on a well-lived life for everything to boil down to this. Cassidy could relate a little too well.

"I'll stay with her for a while. It's my day off, so it should be fine."

That was awfully nice of him. Above and beyond. The extra mile. Cassidy supposed that was just the kind of man he was. That was the kind of man Ty was also, a realization that hadn't gone unnoticed or unappreciated.

"I have a few things to do," Cassidy said. "Maybe I can come give you a break for a while."

Clemson gave her a pointed look, too easily reading between the lines. "If you confront Ernestine about the journal, it's not going to help her health."

His warning echoed in her mind. "I get it."

"I know you want a reason for why she did it. But I also know she's been obsessed with Elsa's death since it happened. She would do anything to get answers."

"I understand." And she did. But that didn't mean Cassidy didn't still want to ask Ernestine why. Telling about the journal hadn't been a wise move—and

Cassidy had trusted her. She supposed that had been her first mistake.

She was also curious about how Clemson knew her so well and why he was so protective. This wasn't the time to ask.

"I'll call you later with any updates." Creases formed as he frowned. "Okay?"

"Okay," Cassidy said. "Thanks, Clemson."

In the meantime, Cassidy would keep looking for answers.

———

Feeling a renewed urge to keep investigating, Cassidy left Ernestine's place and stopped at the library.

Yes, the library.

Mostly because she'd heard that the Friends of the Library were having a meeting and looking for new members. This just might be the perfect time for Cassidy to volunteer, make connections, and ask questions.

The group easily welcomed her into their little circle, thrilled for some fresh blood. Today's goal: separate donated books by genre for an upcoming sale. Cassidy could handle that.

The room they were working in was a decent size— almost as big as the library itself. Apparently, various civic groups used it, and the town had taken that into consideration before building. The library itself utilized its space well with high ceilings, shelves filled to the brim with books, comfortable-looking orange couches, and various tables and work stations.

Cassidy chose the table where Vivian Bozeman just happened to be working.

The woman surprised her—at least, on first impression. She was petite with a demure demeanor, the kind of person who could easily be overlooked because of her mousy disposition. The brunette was neatly dressed with her hair pulled into a tight bun.

She seemed way too sweet for someone like Bozeman.

Cassidy needed to think of a way to strike up a conversation.

"I just loved this one." Cassidy held up a well-used paperback novel by Sue Grafton.

Vivian stopped sorting long enough to smile at Cassidy. "I used to have an affinity for mystery novels. I read them as quickly as some women eat a box of chocolates."

"What changed that?" Cassidy took a deep breath, the dusty scent of old books filling her senses. Lucy would have loved that smell—she was a musician and a reader whereas Cassidy had been an academic and athlete. Her mind tried to wander back to those memories, but she stopped herself. One problem at a time.

"I married a cop," Vivian said. "Suddenly every bad scenario in those books became real-life scenarios that could happen to my husband."

Cassidy shuffled through a couple more books, trying to imagine caring that much about Bozeman. She couldn't. But it was nice that he did have someone who was concerned for him. Everyone needed a support system—especially an incompetent cop who might be a potential killer.

"That makes sense. So, you're Chief Bozeman's wife?"

Vivian offered another brief smile, but it didn't quite reach her eyes. "I am."

"Are you from this area?" Cassidy tried to sound casual, even though eagerness tried to creep in behind her words.

Vivian paused with a steamy romance novel in her hands. "No, I came down here from New Jersey to work for the summer while I was in college. Like so many people, I decided to stay. I actually met Alan when he moved here several years later to become the police chief."

"Sounds like there's a good story in there." Cassidy rubbed her nose, trying to stave off a sneeze. Some of these books were old, with yellowed pages, creased spines, and bent covers. The dust from years of storage was starting to get to her.

Vivian went back to sorting, an obvious melancholy washing over her. "I always wanted a good love story. The truth is, Alan and I were fixed up. We were engaged six months later, and we married a year after we first met."

"That doesn't sound all that bad. It's actually a very sweet story." It made Bozeman seem halfway human.

"I didn't say it was all bad. It just wasn't exciting." She offered a wispy-looking grin.

"Sometimes we women don't need exciting. We need stable, right?"

"I suppose." Vivian paused long enough to answer a question another member had for her. Then she turned back to Cassidy and continued sorting. "It's just a shame he's been so preoccupied lately. It's easy to feel second string, you know?"

Cassidy raised her eyebrows, surprised—but grateful—that Vivian had opened up so easily. "Yeah, I do know. I called off an engagement before for that very reason. Why has he been preoccupied? Is it that stressful being police chief here? It seems like a pretty peaceful town."

Her words veered on the edge of an interrogation, and Cassidy tried to pull her tone back. Instead, she concentrated on sorting more novels—some well-read and others appearing brand new, spines unbroken.

"His grandmother has been ill for the last year. Poor lady."

Cassidy blinked in surprise. She hadn't expected to hear that. It made Bozeman actually seem even more human. It was easier to think of him as a one-dimensional character instead.

"Has she?" Cassidy said. "I'm sorry to hear that."

"It's not even physically that she's been suffering," Vivian said. "It's mental. She's been acting out of her mind. She'll be depressed one minute, and the next she's bouncing off the walls, spending money, and acting erratically."

"That has to be difficult." Cassidy's roommate in college had suffered with mental illness, so she'd seen firsthand how devastating it could be. Thankfully, Sandra—her roommate—had managed to control the underlying problems with the right mix of drugs, counseling, and lifestyle changes.

"It's even more difficult because she won't stay on her meds," Vivian continued. "They're the only thing that seem to keep her grounded. But, wow, are they expensive."

"That's never good, is it?" Meds? Was Bozeman knee-deep in this so he could pay medical expenses? It seemed like a possibility—a weak one, but Cassidy would keep an open mind.

Vivian shook her head, her lips pulled into a tight line. "Alan drives up to Raleigh once a week to see her. It's quite the trip, but it's important she have that support system."

"Doesn't she have anyone else who could help?"

"Alan is the only grandchild. And you probably know that his father is in politics and is busy—too busy. So that just leaves Alan. He's the one she prefers anyway."

"Do you go with him?"

Vivian chuckled lightly. "No, not with her being in her current state. I'll just upset her when she's already cantankerous. She really only likes to see Alan."

"I see."

"I know it sounds funny. But it's better that way." Vivian tossed a paperback into another pile.

"I imagine it's hard for him to get away with his job."

"It is. But he manages to go every Wednesday."

Wednesdays? That was the night the deals usually went down at the Point. Did that mean he was out of town for that event? Did that clear him as a suspect?

"Listen to me." Vivian rolled her eyes. "I'm talking way too much. But you're such a good listener."

Sometimes being a good listener paid off.

CHAPTER
TWENTY-ONE

BACK IN HER CAR, Cassidy's secret phone rang. She saw that it was Samuel and quickly answered.

"Did you get the package?" He cut through the formalities and jumped right to business.

"I did." Cassidy started her car and lowered the windows to let a breeze in. "Thanks for sending it."

"Anything interesting?"

She remembered those memos. She hated feeling pulled in two different directions, but that was exactly how she felt. Getting Ty out of jail was her first priority, but she couldn't stop thinking about Lucy either—especially when new evidence seemed to be emerging.

"There was one thing," Cassidy started. "Samuel, the memos were addressed to someone with the name Tango Mango."

"Okay."

She glanced out the window, looking for any sign of trouble, but she saw nothing other than two teens riding their bikes on the sidewalk. "Does anyone know who that is?"

"Not to my knowledge. We're still trying to figure out who all is involved. We believe this Tango Mango person is the one who developed this strand of flakka. As you know, it was manufactured in a lab, and there are many forms of the drug. DH-7's form is the most potent, and it keeps evolving into something more dangerous and deadly. Of course, users are getting a bigger high, and that's all they care about."

Cassidy sucked in a breath as she processed that. Things were making more sense than she wanted to acknowledge. Because if the pieces she was putting together in her head were true . . . then she was going to have to face a reality she'd rather she didn't.

"What's going on, Cassidy?" Samuel's voice hitched lower.

"Tango Mango is what my friend Lucy's dad used to call her." She almost didn't want to say the words, but she did anyway. This might be her one opportunity to have this conversation.

"That's unusual but nothing definitive."

She nibbled the inside of her lip a moment, contemplating what she would say next. Her frayed nerves simmered in the midday heat. "No, but Samuel, her father owns a huge pharmaceutical company that develops and manufactures drugs."

When Samuel spoke again, his tone changed from skeptical to validating. "I'll see what I can find out for you. That's enough to warrant a look, at least."

"Thanks, Samuel."

"You staying low-key there?" A mild warning etched his voice.

Cassidy remembered everything that had happened over the past couple days. Low-key wouldn't accurately describe her life. But she already had too many irons in the fire, as the saying went, to explain her current situation—especially since it had nothing to do with DH-7.

She cleared her throat. "I'm trying to."

"There's a rumor around here that DH-7 is fracturing."

Her breath caught at his words. "That's great news."

"I know. I just hope it's true. I'll keep you updated."

No sooner had Cassidy hung up with Samuel did her other phone ring. Her heart skipped a beat at the name on her screen. It was Del, Ty's mom.

The woman felt like a mother to Cassidy, even texting her daily with little snippets about life.

But Del hardly ever called.

Cassidy put the phone to her ear and plastered on a cheerful voice. "Hi, Del."

"Cassidy! It's so good to hear your voice. It's been too long." Del's voice sounded bubbly and warm on the other line.

"It has been. I agree. How are you doing?"

Her jovial voice dipped. "I've got to be honest. It's been rough these past couple of weeks, Cassidy."

Her heart panged with compassion. Cassidy couldn't imagine everything the woman was going through. "I'm so sorry to hear that. I've been praying for you."

"I appreciate that more than you know." Del paused. "Listen, I've been trying to catch up with Ty, but I haven't been able to. Is he with you?"

Cassidy's mind raced. She couldn't tell Del that Ty was in jail. It would just add more stress to an already stressful time.

"He's not with me now." Cassidy closed her eyes as a weight pressed on her chest. "I can have him call you. I know he's been super busy lately with the construction at Hope House and things."

"Yes, I know he is. And I hate to bother him. But I really do need to talk to him."

Something about the way Del said the words caused Cassidy to doubt. "Is everything okay?"

"It's . . . it's going to be fine."

Cassidy's breath caught. "Del?"

"The treatment isn't working, and the cancer has spread. I'm going to need surgery. It's pretty involved. I need to let him know." Del's voice cracked.

This was bigger than she wanted to let on, Cassidy realized. More serious. Higher stakes.

"When is the surgery?"

"Next week."

Next week? Would Ty be out of jail by next week? Cassidy would hope so. But she really had no idea. It was all wishful thinking at this point.

"I'll talk to him and make sure he calls you, okay? No worries. Everything is going to be okay."

"I know it will be. Thanks so much, sweetie. I'll talk to you again soon."

But as Cassidy hung up, her heart was heavier than ever.

———

Cassidy went to the Crazy Chefette to grab a bite to eat and update the gang on what was going on.

Her conversation with Del lay heavy on her mind. Should she rush to the station and talk to Ty now?

No, she decided. She'd already been once, and they probably wouldn't let her see him again.

She could call him and share the information . . . but this seemed like a conversation she should have face-to-face.

She wasn't sure what to do, but prayed she'd have the right opening.

It was already well past lunch time when she arrived at the Crazy Chefette, and Cassidy was famished. But she'd been getting phone calls and texts all day from various friends. It was best if she updated them all at once.

Surprisingly, they were all available—or, better yet, they made themselves available.

Lisa was already there—of course. Everyone else showed up ten minutes later once they got Cassidy's message. After ordering fish tacos with an orange jalapeno salsa, Cassidy drew in a deep breath, preparing herself to plunge into all the details.

But, first, she glanced around.

The place was only half full. In the summer, there was usually a line out the door. But now it had dwindled to mostly locals and some fishermen.

Her gaze searched each table. She didn't see anyone suspicious. More like, she didn't see Ed Kyle. But she needed to keep her eyes wide open for the man.

"You look rough, Cassidy." Austin studied her face. "What happened?"

She shrugged, remembering last night's events. "It's been a rough week."

"Did someone do that to you?" Wes squinted, studying her face.

Cassidy let out a breath, knowing it was useless to deny it. "Yeah, someone was hiding in my house last night."

Wes muttered something she couldn't make out—but he sounded angry.

"You should call us, Cassidy." The muscles on Austin's face flexed with restrained emotion. "We're Ty's friends, but we're your friends too. We can be there to help you."

"I appreciate that," Cassidy said. "I really do. But I had no idea this case was going to cause this kind of trouble for me." She took a long sip of water.

"You should stay with someone else tonight," Skye said. She'd hardly touched her salad. She felt things deeply, and her eyes were brimming with unspoken secrets, it seemed.

"I have Kujo. And I'll call if I need help."

The truth was she didn't want to pull either of the ladies into this mess. Too many people had already been hurt.

"Let us help you, Cassidy." Austin stared at her, his eyes dead serious. "That's what friends are for."

His words gripped her heart, and Cassidy realized she could use their help. "There is something you can do . . . are any of you free about nine o'clock tonight?"

———

Ty leaned against the wall of his tiny cell.

The first day here had been bearable. The second day, he'd gotten antsy. Today, he felt like he could lose his mind.

He needed to get out there. He needed to help Cassidy.

Instead, he was facing life in prison for a crime he didn't commit.

He closed his eyes as reality continued to sink in, bit by painful bit.

He trusted that God was in control, but this whole situation had thrown him into a tailspin. Other than praying—which was powerful—he felt helpless.

Not to mention the fact that being alone with his thoughts for so long had released memories he usually tried to avoid by staying busy.

Memories of being in the Middle East. Of watching one of the men under him step on a land mine. Of finding him blown apart.

Ty had rushed to him. Had tried to offer him some kind of hope in his last moments.

But he'd known Goldman wouldn't survive. No one would survive an explosion like that.

The worst part was that Ty had ordered him to go in that direction while Ty had walked the opposite way. If he hadn't done that, Goldman would be alive right now, and Ty would have been the one to die.

That realization haunted him every waking day.

No one should have died on his watch.

Like currents coming from two different directions, his thoughts moved from Goldman to Robby . . . his little brother. He'd been caught up in the drug culture and had walked away from the family. They hadn't seen or heard from him in five years. Five long years.

His mom's heart had been broken. She was going through her first fight with cancer during that time.

Even back then, Ty had felt helpless. He hated the feeling. He was a fighter. A doer. A protector. Yet he'd let down the people who meant the most to him.

Just as he was letting down Cassidy now.

He jerked his head up as the door leading to the cell block opened. Part of him hoped to see Cassidy, though he knew that wouldn't be the case. He was only allowed one visitor a day.

Instead, Quinton led another man inside. "You've got a roommate."

He opened the door and shoved the man into Ty's cell.

"Have fun," Quinton said with a smirk.

The man's entire body looked tense, and every time he breathed, a small growl seemed to escape with the air from his lungs.

This guy was trouble.

Why in the world had Quinton put him in here with Ty instead of in the cell beside him? It was empty.

Unless he wanted to teach Ty a lesson.

His body tensed at the thought of it.

His cellmate paced the dirty floor, his eyes never leaving Ty. Ty remained silent, giving the man his space. He didn't want any trouble, and this man screamed the definition of the word.

"I heard some guy talking down at the docks," the man finally said, stopping his frantic pacing and standing in front of Ty. "He was telling us that he has plans for your girlfriend."

Anger surged up Ty's spine. "What do you mean?"

The man shrugged. "Didn't give details. He just seemed awfully excited about something that was supposed to go down tonight."

The next instant, Ty had the man by his shirt, and he pressed him against the bars. "Tell me everything you know."

The man raised his hands. "I'm just a drunk. I don't know much."

"Who was this guy?"

"Never seen him before. Said he was running from the police."

Was this the guy who'd beat up Cassidy? He was

the only one who made sense. He needed to tell Quinton to go down to the docks and arrest the man.

Ty let go of his cellmate and began banging against the bars. "Quinton. I need you!"

But no one came.

"Oh, yeah. There was one other thing," the man said.

Ty turned toward him, his heart thumping out of control at the possibility of something happening to Cassidy. "What's that?"

"He told me to tell you thank you for taking the fall for all of this." The man's fist connected with Ty's jaw.

———

Cassidy pulled up to Ernestine's place. She had a few hours to kill before she met Austin and Wes to stake out the Point. Clemson's car was still here also.

She wished she could talk to Mac, but he'd gotten stuck in a traffic jam up near DC and would be getting back later than he'd thought. He'd texted her to let her know. She was going to have to continue going solo today.

She knocked on Ernestine's door, and the town's doctor answered a moment later.

"Cassidy, you did come back," he said, blocking the doorway.

"I was hoping to chat with Ernestine."

"She just fell asleep," he said.

Cassidy nodded, feeling her lungs deflate. "I see."

"I don't think she has anything to tell you. She made a judgment call. It was wrong. End of story. Talking to her isn't going to prove anything."

"I understand what you're saying." There was no need to argue because it was obvious his mind was already made up. Yet Cassidy wanted more, wanting to hear it from Ernestine herself. "Is she doing okay?"

Clemson nodded. "I think she'll be fine. But, as you can imagine, she's shaken up."

"If you don't mind me asking, how do you know her so well?"

He smiled sadly. "Believe it or not, we've been writing each other letters for the past six months."

"Letters?" Cassidy hadn't expected that.

"That's right. We can't exactly meet for coffee. So we write each other, and now we feel like old friends. I think it's helped both of us heal from the losses in our lives—for me, my wife. For Ernestine, Elsa."

"That's sweet." She squeezed Clemson's arm. "Tell her she's in my prayers."

Clemson nodded. "I'll do that."

With that door closed, Cassidy headed back to her house. She needed to let Kujo out.

She remained on the deck while Kujo trotted across the beach within sight. Her thoughts turned over and over. She not only needed to track down the person responsible for what had happened, but she needed to be able to prove it.

And that was the tricky part.

Wheezer . . . he was looking for other jobs.

Quinton . . . he was still on the table as a suspect, as far as she was concerned.

Bozeman was at the top of her suspect list. But she needed something concrete to prove it.

Anxiety churned in her stomach. She hated feeling powerless. She hated that Ty was in jail. She still needed to tell him about his mom, but he only got one visit or call a day.

And what about everything with Lucy? What did Tango Mango mean?

Could Lucy's father really be developing flakka for DH-7? Was that the reason Lucy had been killed?

It was seeming more and more likely.

Cassidy never would have suspected that something that had happened ten years ago would somehow be entwined with the current DH-7 crisis in her life.

Again, she remembered how odd it was that she'd been chosen for this assignment, though.

What if there was a bigger plan at stake, one bigger than Cassidy wanted to acknowledge? What if everything somehow tied together?

She wasn't sure how that would be the case. She wasn't even sure if she'd be able to figure it all out until she was able to go back to Seattle. But the answers were getting closer. She didn't like the conclusions she was drawing, but at least she was getting closer to a conclusion.

CHAPTER
TWENTY-TWO

TY QUICKLY RECOVERED from the blow to his jaw. He rose to full height and raised his arms, ready to defend himself. When the man swung again, Ty blocked the punch.

Two seconds later, he swept his leg around the man, striking his knees. The man hit the floor, taken by surprise.

The next instant, the doors opened, and Quinton came running in. He unlocked the cell and pulled Ty's new roommate from the space.

"What are you doing?" Quinton demanded.

"I was defending myself since this man punched me." Ty rubbed his jaw.

"He came at me first," the man said, his voice taking on a whiny sound.

"Check the camera footage." Ty bristled. "You'll see that's not true."

Quinton jerked the man into the cell next to Ty's,

still scowling at Ty the whole time. "All I know is that this guy will be gone in the morning once the alcohol wears off. I can't say the same for you."

Ty narrowed his eyes, not liking where this was going.

"You know you're not getting out of here, right?" Quinton came back over to Ty's cell once the other man was secure.

"I didn't do anything wrong."

"That's what every criminal says." Quinton smirked. "I guess your little girlfriend will be left out there on her own, needing a new shoulder to cry on."

Pressure built inside Ty. As much as he tried to hold his anger at bay, it was useless. Quinton was goading him, and it was working.

"What does that mean?" Ty asked between clenched teeth.

"She's pretty. I'm sure she won't be lonely for long."

Ty stepped closer to the bars separating them. "Leave her alone."

"She did have dinner with me this week." Quinton grinned, satisfaction in his gaze. "I guess she needed something to occupy her time."

"I'm sure it wasn't social."

"You'll never know, will you?" Quinton smiled again, not bothering to hide his dislike for Ty.

Ty fisted his hands and reminded himself that taking the bait wouldn't help his situation. Instead, he remained silent until Quinton finally realized his fun was over.

"Anyway, have a nice evening," Quinton said, walking away. "Tomorrow, you'll be gone from here and in with the big boys."

"What does that mean?" Ty said.

Quinton paused. "You didn't hear?"

"Hear what?"

"A space opened up in the county jail," he said. "Bozeman is going to transfer you there himself tomorrow."

———

Cassidy took another sip of her coffee and leaned back in her seat. She knew she could do this stakeout alone, but she also knew it wouldn't be wise. Austin and Wes would be great assets if anything happened. And they were willing—more than willing—to help her out. Ty would approve of this.

Austin had insisted on driving to the Point. They'd taken his quad cab truck. Cassidy sat in the back seat, and she'd packed enough snacks for all of them.

They'd parked in the woods near the lighthouse and were now waiting to see if anything was going down here tonight. This could be the first clue as to what was taking place and who was behind it.

This was the first time Cassidy had ever hung out with just Austin and Wes. They'd gotten together plenty of times with the rest of the gang to eat dinner or play volleyball, and she knew they were both upstanding kinds of guys.

But it was hard to be on a stakeout with them without revealing who she really was. Being a fake was entirely exhausting. She wished she could be truthful, but it was too big a risk.

"How does Ty seem to be doing?" Austin asked, staring straight ahead with an intensity that surprised Cassidy.

"He seemed a little discouraged this morning." Cassidy frowned as the words left her lips. "That's why I have to come up with answers here."

"He's the most honorable guy I know." Wes popped a peanut into his mouth. "He wouldn't have done this."

"I know your support means a lot to him," Cassidy poked her head between the seats so she could see the shoreline more easily. "I'm not sure how everything is going to go down here, guys."

"You've been really into this investigation thing, haven't you?" Wes glanced back, his eyebrows drawing upward.

Both of these guys were really great, she realized. It seemed too cliché to ask—so she didn't—but she wondered why they were single. Why they'd come here. What they'd left behind.

Everyone here on Lantern Beach seemed to have a story. Austin and Wes probably weren't any different.

Maybe when Bible study started back up in a couple of weeks, she would learn more.

"Wheezer is thinking about moving." She tucked her leg beneath her and tried to settle in for the conversation. "He thinks something bad is going down here.

According to Vivian—Bozeman's wife—Bozeman is spending his free time up in Raleigh visiting his grandma. That leaves Quinton."

"I'm not sure he's smart enough for any of this," Austin said. "He used to surf with me a few times. All he really thinks about is women. The man has no common sense."

"Yeah, I had that impression. But whoever did this set up Ty. He must have really been thinking this through because not only was that paper left at the scene with Ty's name, but a gun was also planted, as well as Cullum's keys."

"So, it's someone with skills and resources." Austin leaned back and let out a deep breath.

"I'd say so," Cassidy said. "Whoever it is hired that Ed guy who came to my place last night."

"You haven't seen him today, have you?" Wes asked.

"Thank goodness—no. But there's a chance he's still around. The person behind this must think I'm getting too close to the answers, and he's trying to silence me." She stared out at the shoreline, waiting for some kind of clue about what was going on.

Did this all go back to drugs . . . again? It seemed like all the crimes on the island somehow went back to drugs. The rugged coastland offered privacy and isolation. The waters offered easy transportation. That made it perfect for illegal activities—and Cassidy had seen plenty of them since coming to the area.

Were the police turning a blind eye to everything going on? Did they not care? Maybe they were getting a kickback or didn't have enough resources to fight it. She didn't know.

Just then, Cassidy pointed across the shoreline. Lights bounced in the darkness. Movement signaled some kind of change. Activity. "Look, something is going on over there!"

"There sure is." Austin sat up straighter.

"And, what do you know?" Wes muttered. "One of those guys is wearing a police uniform."

CHAPTER
TWENTY-THREE

THE THREE OF them climbed from the truck and crept along the edge of the forest toward the scene. There were three men out there. One had driven a truck onto the shore, and the others had gotten off a boat. Cassidy would guess the cop had driven the truck.

She paused behind a tree, thankful that the darkness concealed them. From the shadows, Cassidy eyeballed the scene. As much as she wished she recognized the vehicle or the silhouettes, she didn't. It could be anyone out there. It was too dark to make out any details.

The waves and the leaves clattering in the breeze were just loud enough to mask any of the conversation. From where her team stood, they weren't going to find out anything. The last thing Cassidy wanted was to leave here with more questions.

But that was what it looked like she'd be doing.

The men—she assumed they were men—huddled close together. Something was exchanged between them, a small package of some sort. And five minutes later, it was over.

The boat pulled away, and the officer started walking back to his truck.

"This is our time, guys," Cassidy whispered. "We've got to move in. Now."

"I'll take the left side," Austin said.

"Cassidy and I will take the right side." Wes eyed the beach, as if he didn't want to miss anything.

They moved closer to the scene. Cassidy watched the officer, wishing she could see more. But she couldn't. He was still too far away.

As he reached his truck, his figure finally came into focus.

She blanched at whom she saw.

Quinton.

"We need to talk to him," Cassidy muttered, ready for action. "Before he leaves."

"Let's go," Wes said.

Together, they darted from behind the trees toward Quinton. The sand concealed their footsteps, and the darkness shadowed their approaching figures.

It wasn't until they were three feet away from Quinton that he had a clue they were there.

He froze like a deer in the headlights before glancing around as if considering the possibility of darting.

"We need to talk," Cassidy said, her voice unyielding.

———

"What are you doing here?" Quinton growled, lowering his voice and leaning toward them.

"The question is: what are *you* doing here?" Austin asked. "It looks rather illegal."

Quinton glanced over his shoulder, as if looking for anyone who might be watching. "You could ruin it all."

"Define all," Cassidy said.

"I've been trying to bust these guys for the past eight months." His teeth were clenched as he said the words, even though the guys in the boat were long gone.

"Bust them?" Wes let out a hard chuckle. "You look like you're one of them."

"That's the point," Quinton seethed. "They do think I'm one of them."

"You should start from the beginning before I call the authorities," Cassidy said. "And I'm not talking about the Lantern Beach PD."

"Cool your jets." Quinton wiped his brow. "We all need to take a step back and calm down. I'm trying to figure out who's calling the shots within this little business going on here. I've been doing an undercover sting to find answers."

"What are you talking about?" Austin said, sounding truly confused.

The story did sound far-fetched.

"These guys have been doing drug deals out here for the past six months," Quinton said. "Mostly recreational stuff. We're trying to figure out who's behind it."

"Why don't you just arrest those guys you're meeting with?" Wes asked.

"Because that doesn't cut off the head." Quinton scowled. "We need to figure out the supplier."

That might be true but . . . "Why are you dressed like a cop if you're undercover?"

His nostrils flared as his frustration rose. "Because everyone around here knows I'm a cop." His words came out rushed and rapid. "There was no need to try and hide it. So I'm acting like a dirty cop with a bad habit. So far, they've bought it. As long as they get theirs, they're happy."

Cassidy supposed that could be true. But it could also very easily be a way of covering up his involvement. After her experience in DH-7, Quinton's story made more sense, however.

Being undercover was precarious.

"If your story is true, why are you letting this go on for eight months? You haven't been able to find any answers yet?" Cassidy watched his expression, looking for any signs of deceit.

She saw nothing.

"I'm doing my best, but I don't want to rush the process." Quinton narrowed his eyes again and rubbed his jaw. "I don't want to get myself killed. Besides, once I find out who's behind this, I tell the NCSBI. I'll let them step in. I can't take them down on my own."

Cassidy supposed his story made sense. But she still had more questions.

She stepped closer—close enough to see the flecks in his eyes. "Why didn't you tell me Ed Kyle got away?"

Quinton's eyes widened with surprise. "Bozeman said he was going to tell you."

"Wheezer said that you said *you* were going to tell me." This conversation was giving Cassidy a headache.

"I started out to do that when Bozeman stopped me. I don't know what happened."

"Wait a minute," Cassidy said. "How did this guy even get away?"

"It happened at the police station. I pulled him out of the back of my squad car. Somehow, he'd gotten out of the handcuffs. He took off."

"And you couldn't catch him?" Wes didn't bother to hide the outrage in his voice.

Quinton's eyes narrowed with insult. "No. It took me off guard. I started after him, but a car pulled up and he jumped inside."

"And then?"

"And then we searched the island. But we couldn't find him. We think he somehow got off the island."

"That's . . . unfortunate." Cassidy's jaw clenched. And it was another example of the police department's incompetence. She wanted to give them a chance. She really did. But it was just so hard when they constantly messed up.

"I know. Believe me, I know." He shifted. Glanced around. Let out a sigh. "Here's the other strange thing. I don't know how someone knew to be at the police station to pick him up."

He had Cassidy's attention now. "What do you mean?"

"I mean, it was like someone knew he was going to escape and was waiting for him. And I just can't understand how that's possible."

Cassidy had an idea on how it was possible. It was because of Bozeman. He had to be the one behind this. And there was one way she could think to prove it.

"Quinton, you need to think this through. Listen to what you're saying. Something isn't right here."

He shrugged. "Yeah, I get that."

"You could be the hero here. You could save the day. Figure out what's going on."

"What do you mean?"

Cassidy swallowed hard. "Quinton . . . the gun that was found at Ty's house didn't belong to him. Did you guys trace that back to the original owner?"

He shrugged. "I'm sure the chief did. I'm sure it came back as Ty's."

"You should look into it," Cassidy said. "Because it wasn't Ty's gun. See if you can find out whose it actually is. It didn't appear out of thin air, either."

His eyes widened with realization. "You're probably just lying for him."

"I'm not. I promise you, I'm not."

"So you're telling me Ty really is innocent? You're sure he was set up?"

Cassidy nodded, a surge of hope rushing through her. "That's exactly what I'm telling you. If you can figure out who the real bad guy is, you'll be the star of the police force and finally get some of that recognition you deserve."

He pursed his lips in thought before nodding. "Maybe I'll look into it. But I'm not making any promises."

TWENTY-FOUR

AFTER QUINTON LEFT, Austin, Wes, and Cassidy remained there at the beach, standing with the lighthouse towering behind them in the background.

There was no one else out here, and they needed to talk. What better place than on these secluded shores?

"Let's say it's Bozeman who's behind this," Austin said. "He's the only one who makes sense. But how do we prove anything?"

"We need motive, means, and opportunity." Cassidy paused as she realized how she sounded and shrugged innocently. "At least, that's what I hear from reading my crime novels."

How much longer would her friends buy that? Or did they even buy it now? She wasn't sure.

Thankfully, neither Austin or Wes said anything.

"Would the motive be drugs?" Austin asked, his dark, curly hair blowing in his face.

Cassidy shook her head. "Drugs are rarely the

motive in themselves, unless you're dealing with a user who needs another hit. Usually it's about money."

Austin and Wes stared at her, neither saying anything for a minute.

Finally, she shrugged. "That's my guess, at least."

"So let's say Bozeman needs the money," Wes said. "Why? He lives a pretty humble existence. I've been in his house to fix a leaky toilet. The place is nothing fancy. They don't have nice cars or take lavish vacations."

"Maybe he's in debt," Austin suggested. "Or maybe he's been blackmailed. But even if either of those things were true, I don't know how we would figure that out."

These two were better at this investigating thing than she'd thought.

"We have no way of seeing his bank records, but his wife did tell me he's taking care of his grandmother and her medications are expensive. I don't know if they're expensive enough to warrant all this."

"True," Wes agreed. "Bozeman could probably ask his father for help in covering some of those expenses, if it came down to it."

"Which would really only leave word of mouth to figure out his money situation," Cassidy said. "I doubt very many people in Bozeman's inner circle would spill that kind of information."

Austin nodded slowly, his eyes steady and focused. "That's probably true. Let's say that is Bozeman's motive. We know he had the means and opportunity. He could have easily killed that guy, just like Elsa hinted at in her journal. No doubt he was at the costume party at some point that night—probably working it. He saw Ty in the police uniform and knew he'd be the perfect scapegoat. He wrote Ty's information down on that slip of paper, put it in the Ziploc, and left it by the body."

"As a matter of fact, I remember seeing Bozeman there that night," Wes said, a memory lighting his gaze. "He and his wife were dressed up like Andy Griffith and Barney Fife."

Cassidy smiled when she thought about Vivian dressed like Barney Fife. It would have been . . . cute. Her thoughts quickly went back to the investigation.

"As soon as the body was discovered, maybe Bozeman went into hyper-drive," Cassidy added, picturing everything playing out in her mind. "He took the gun, planted it at Ty's place, along with McGrath's keys. I'm sure it seemed like a foolproof plan. And now Ty's facing life in prison."

Austin's hands went to his hips. "Even if all of this is true, how do we prove it?"

"That's a great question . . ." Wes muttered.

Silence stretched between them a moment, and each seemed to be lost in their own thoughts. There was a lot to think about. Too much, it seemed.

"The air feels different, doesn't it?" Austin glanced around.

"You think we'll get a bad storm around here this year?" Cassidy asked, realizing how mundane the question seemed considering everything going on around them. Yet her thoughts needed a break, needed a reboot.

"We're due for another one. It wouldn't surprise me. Although we did have a pretty bad hurricane last year, so we'll see." He glanced at Austin. "You remember when that actress was here and helped bust that crime ring?"

"Who can forget about it? It was the talk of the town."

That sounded like a story for another day.

Since Cassidy had arrived, there had been several offshore storms. She was lucky she hadn't experienced any extreme weather since she'd arrived, but fall was coming. That was when hurricane season kicked into full gear. She felt like there had been a storm approaching in her life for a long time.

"That makes me think about something Ty told me," Cassidy said. "He was telling me how to get out of a riptide. He said the mistake most people make is they try to swim against the current and exhaust themselves."

"It's true," Wes said. "I've tried it before, and it's not pretty. You use up all your energy until you can't fight it anymore."

"I've been thinking about this investigation. Maybe I've been approaching it too much like someone caught in a rip current. I've been fighting the stream of water, and I'm only getting exhausted."

"What do you suggest?" Wes asked. "How do you get to safety?"

"Well, Ty also said that you should swim out of the

current—horizontal to the shore—and then swim back. Correct?"

"That's right." Wes stared at her, as if waiting to see where she was going with this.

"I'm going to go above the authorities. Above Bozeman, at least. I'm going to call the State Bureau of Investigation and get them involved." It might mean breaking her cover, but she'd do what she had to. She'd do it for Ty.

"Cops don't like accusations against the brotherhood," Austin said.

"You're right," Cassidy said. "But it's the only thing I can do here. I have a contact there. Agent Dan Peterson. I'm going to call him and see if he'll meet me here."

If she blew her cover, she blew her cover. She didn't care right now.

"It seems risky," Wes said.

Cassidy's phone rang before this conversation could continue any longer. Deny it too much, and they'd only get suspicious.

She didn't recognize the number on her screen, but she answered anyway.

"Cassidy, it's me."

She stiffened at the familiar voice. "Ty?"

He sounded urgent. "Cassidy, Quinton informed me earlier that they're transferring me to the county jail tomorrow."

Alarm raced through her. "What? Why?"

"I guess there was an opening." Ty paused. "But

here's the thing—Bozeman himself is going to transfer me."

Cassidy sucked in a deep breath. She didn't like the sound of that. Not at all.

She needed to make that phone call to the State Bureau of Investigation as soon as she got back to her place.

Cassidy knew she needed to tell Ty about his mom, as well, though she dreaded breaking the news—especially like this. But she braced herself and did it anyway. He needed to know as soon as possible.

———

Fifteen minutes later, Austin pulled up to Cassidy's place and insisted on checking it out for her. She wasn't going to argue—not after everything that had happened.

But once in her driveway, Austin didn't immediately make a move to get out. Cassidy sensed he had something on his mind.

"Ty really likes you, Cass," Austin said.

"Good. I like him too."

"I don't want to see him hurt." He paused and drummed his hands on the steering wheel a minute. "I've always had the impression you may not stick around here."

Cassidy appreciated that he was looking out for Ty. Yet the weight on her chest only felt heavier at his words. "The last thing I want to do is hurt Ty."

Austin nodded. "Good. I'm glad to hear that. He's .. . well, he's been through a lot."

"I know. Believe me, I do. And as far as me sticking around . . . Ty knows what my intentions for the future are. We're on the same page."

He held up his fist and waited for her to hit her knuckles against his. "Cool. I just had to check."

"It's good to have people who watch your back." She opened her door. "Now let's check my place out."

But when she stepped out of her car, a peculiar smell hit her.

Smoke.

Why was she smelling smoke?

She glanced over at Ty's place and saw the first flicker of light.

Of fire.

"It's the new addition . . ." Austin muttered, following her gaze. "Call 911."

As Cassidy pulled out her phone, Austin darted toward the back of the house. He found a hose and cranked the water on. Then he rushed to try and put out the flames.

Thankfully, the flickers on the outside walls were still small right now. But that could change with one shift of the wind.

How could someone have done this? Wasn't it bad enough that Ty was already in jail? But now they had to destroy his hard work?

The dispatcher promised to send fire trucks ASAP.

Cassidy prayed they got there in time. Almost as soon as Cassidy hung up, a sound caught her ear.

Was that . . . Kujo?

Cassidy's blood pressure skyrocketed. Had someone put Kujo in Ty's house before setting it on fire? Because those barks weren't coming from her own cottage. Cassidy was sure of it.

"I've got to make sure Kujo's not up there!" she yelled to Austin before darting up the stairs.

She hurried to the door, grabbed the knob, and twisted it.

It was unlocked. She'd think about that later.

She rushed inside and paused in the smoke-filled living room. "Kujo?"

The barking still sounded, but there was no Kujo.

Covering her mouth with her shirt, she hurried toward the back of the house and opened the first door she came to. The bathroom.

It was empty.

She tried Ty's room and the guest bedroom. Both were also empty.

Where was Kujo?

She still heard him barking.

She stopped at the last bedroom.

The barking definitely sounded like it was coming from inside this room. If not, Cassidy was out of options.

She stepped inside but didn't see the dog.

The closet?

Would someone have really locked him in the closet?

She rushed toward the door and pulled it open.

It was empty.

Except for one thing on the carpet.

A digital recorder . . . playing the sound of a dog barking.

Adrenaline pumped through her blood.

Cassidy had to get out of here. Now. This had all been a trap.

She rushed back toward the door. It was closed.

Closed?

She hadn't closed it.

Cassidy tugged on the handle . . . but it was locked.

As the smoke began invading her lungs, she glanced around. She had to think of another way out of here before the fire consumed her.

CHAPTER
TWENTY-FIVE

CASSIDY BANGED ON THE DOOR. She knew there was little chance of anyone hearing her. The crackle of the fire was getting louder by the moment, and the spray from the water hose would conceal any other sounds.

The room felt like a furnace.

The flames were close. She couldn't see them. But she could feel them licking at the walls, just out of sight.

Had the person who did this—most likely Ed Kyle—stayed behind, just waiting for Cassidy to come looking for Kujo?

He must have.

It was just another way of trying to silence her. Of injuring her.

Or was he trying to kill her?

She couldn't let that happen.

Cassidy banged on the door again but stopped as smoke filled her lungs.

Cassidy coughed, unable to breathe.

This wasn't good.

She ran to the window and tried to throw it open.

It wouldn't budge.

When she glanced at the edges, she saw someone had nailed it shut.

She grabbed the small table beside the bed and raised it over her shoulder. Using all of her strength, she propelled it into the window.

The glass shattered.

She used the legs of the table to remove the lethal shards that remained on the edge of the frame. Then she stuck her head outside, sucking in a quick breath of cleaner air.

The house was on stilts, the kind used on most beach-front cottages here. If Cassidy jumped down—and she would if she had to—she could break bones. It would beat her burning alive in here, though. She'd explore other options first.

"Austin!" she yelled. "Up here! Help!"

Hopefully, the intruder hadn't done anything to him.

But before the idea could settle, Austin appeared on the sand below. Cassidy released her breath. He knew she was up here. *Thank You, Jesus.*

He squinted, as if trying to comprehend what was happening. And then, without asking any questions, he darted toward the front of the house.

The flames permeated the walls now.

It was just a matter of time before this whole room was consumed.

Cassidy ran toward the door and tried to open it again.

The knob burned her hand.

Her heart rate surged. She needed to make some choices.

Fast.

Wait for Austin?

Or jump?

Before she had to make that decision, the door flew open.

Austin grabbed her arm and pulled her from the room and down the stairs to safety.

They stepped outside just as the firetrucks arrived.

———

Ty tried to sleep. But he couldn't. These cells weren't made for sleeping.

Nor could he rest knowing that Bozeman would be escorting him to the county jail tomorrow.

What would happen? How would it play out? An accident on the ferry? Would he claim that Ty fought with him and he'd had no choice but to shoot?

Ty wasn't sure.

But he didn't like where this was going. The thoughts had haunted him all evening. He'd tried to combat them with prayer, but the anxiety crept back in every chance it got.

Wheezer stepped into the holding cell area, and Ty sat up, wondering if he was getting another cellmate.

Instead, Wheezer announced, "You've got a phone call."

His voice sounded regretful.

Ty stood, his muscles taut and on alert. He was only allowed one call a day—although it was past midnight. Still, a bad feeling churned in his gut.

Wheezer escorted him to the phone on the wall across from his cell and stood there while Ty answered.

"Ty, it's me. Cassidy." Her voice sounded strained and maybe even hoarse. "The police made an exception for me to call you again."

Had something else happened to her? His blood felt like it turned to lava at the thought. "What's going on?"

"Ty . . . I don't know how to tell you this. Someone set your house on fire."

"What?" Had Ty even heard her correctly?

"I'm sorry. We tried to put it out."

"We?" What was she saying? She wasn't making any sense.

"Austin and me. He insisted on driving me home to check everything out."

He'd thank Austin for that later . . . if he got the chance. "Are you okay?"

"Everyone's fine," she said. "Kujo included. Your house, though . . ."

"Is it totally destroyed?" He thought about all his memories there. He'd grieve the loss, but stuff was just stuff. It could be replaced.

"It's too early to say. It was mainly the new addition on the back that was hit with the flames. But the water damage from firefighters . . . I just don't know."

"The important thing is that everyone is safe," Ty said. "We can always rebuild."

He had to admit that the setback felt deflating. He'd worked so hard to get Hope House off the ground. Now one person's actions had changed all of that.

"I know. But it's still got to be disappointing." Cassidy paused.

Wheezer motioned for him to get off the phone. His time was up. Maybe in more than one way.

"I love you, Cassidy. I'll see you later. Stay safe. Please stay safe."

———

Cassidy hung up with Ty, her heart heavy. He needed her right now, and she couldn't be there for him.

That didn't feel okay.

She took one last look at Ty's place. With her outside lights on, she could see that the back side was charred yet surprisingly intact. Maybe there was hope that Ty wouldn't have to start anew on his project. Even though insurance should cover some of the damages, he'd be months behind, and Cassidy hated that.

That was assuming he was released from jail, and Bozeman didn't kill him.

"Are you okay?" Austin asked, coming from around the back of Ty's place, where he'd been inspecting it.

Since he was a contractor, he had a better gauge on repairs than she did.

Firefighters were still swarming the area and said they hadn't determined a cause yet.

Cassidy already knew—it was arson.

Cassidy had also reported to Quinton that she'd been locked inside. He'd looked at her in disbelief but had taken her statement.

Cassidy knew one thing for sure: whoever did this hadn't counted on Austin being with her. If he hadn't been . . . Cassidy might not be here right now.

"I'm fine." She crossed her arms and looked up at him. "Did you see anyone out here, Austin?"

They hadn't had the chance to talk since everything happened. Between the fire fighters, police, and paramedics, it had been a whirlwind.

"No, I didn't. Of course, I was focused on putting the flames out. If I hadn't seen the glass fall from the window, I might not have found you. I certainly couldn't hear you above the flames and the spray of the water."

"Thanks again for everything," she muttered.

"Any time." He squeezed her arm. "I'll check in later."

Cassidy went back up to her cottage, her mind swirling from everything that had happened. After she got some sleep, she'd call the North Carolina State Bureau of Investigation and tell them everything.

But for now, she needed to clear her pounding head. She sat on the couch and closed her eyes. Should she tell Samuel what was going on? Probably. He should be in the loop here.

Before she relaxed too much, she picked up the phone and dialed his number.

He didn't answer. And Cassidy didn't leave a message.

But she couldn't help but think how strange it was.

Samuel always answered.

She gripped her phone and tried not to think about worst-case scenarios.

CHAPTER
TWENTY-SIX
22 WEEKS EARLIER

CADY DECIDED TO WAIT.

It may have been the wrong choice. She wasn't sure. Part of her wanted to slink into the crowd on the other side of the door. The other part of her knew it was a chance she couldn't take. If someone saw her, it would all be over.

The flash drive burned in her pocket. She could feel the metal poking into her skin as she sat with her knees pulled to her chest beneath Raul's desk.

She closed her eyes, trying to envision what she wanted her life to look like one day. Once she was done with this assignment.

Would she go back to the way things were? Or was that foolish? Her normal life was gone, wasn't it?

She'd been so honored and so anxious to take this assignment and to prove herself. But what was the cost?

And just why was she chosen for this anyway? The

thought gripped her throat until she felt as if she couldn't breathe.

The inquiry had whispered at her conscience before, but she'd tried to ignore it.

Except now she couldn't.

Of all the people out there, why had a junior level detective covering white-collar crimes, the child of one of the wealthiest couples in the United States, been chosen for this role? She'd grown up with the proverbial silver spoon in her mouth. Even though she'd altered her appearance, she'd been on the cover of newspapers and magazines before.

The choice of her being in this role was . . . questionable.

She hadn't stopped long enough to think about it before. Or maybe she just hadn't *wanted* to think about it. She wasn't sure.

But what if she'd been chosen for a purpose other than bringing down this organization? What if there was more to this?

Her heart raced at the thought.

Think happier thoughts, Cady. Think about life after this.

Okay, so maybe she wouldn't go back to being a Seattle detective. But she could get a job *somewhere* else.

What about Ryan? They were supposed to get married. He loved her . . . didn't he? But could she really see life with him permanently? He was married to his job. He was brisk and professional and . . .

Was that what she wanted?

She closed her eyes again. No, what she wanted one

day was a life different than the one she'd grown up with. Money hadn't been a blessing. No, it had been a god and had ultimately controlled them.

No, Cady wanted a simple life one day. Maybe away from the city.

Could that be true? She'd never thought about it before, but she felt certain at the moment.

And she wanted a family. She didn't want her career to be the center of her existence. Because at the end of her life, her career wouldn't mourn her.

How would she make those changes? She had no idea.

But that was what she needed to do.

And she needed to find Lucy's killer.

But, before she could do any of those things, she needed to get out of here. Turn in the information. And disappear for a while so DH-7 wouldn't track her down.

The noise in the other room began to die down. She glanced at her watch. It was almost 4:00 a.m. She'd been in here for hours.

Had anyone noticed her absence?

Probably not. She'd told them she was going into work.

She'd gotten a part-time job at a twenty-four-hour drugstore as a way of maintaining her cover. She was able to pass messages back and forth to Samuel as a part of her job there.

Sometimes she wondered if Raul had his guys check

up on her there. If he sent his guys to make sure that's what she was really doing.

The man was always suspicious.

An hour later, total silence stretched in the other room.

This was her time.

If Cady was going to get out of here, she had to do it now.

Hesitantly, she crawled out from under the desk. She stretched her legs, her body aching from sitting in the same position for most of the night.

She placed the desk chair back like it was, checked the computer to make sure it still looked the same, and then she went to the door.

She hesitated there for just a minute.

She gripped the silver knob, her hand squeezing the metal in apprehension.

On the count of three, she twisted it. Opened the door only a crack. And she peeked out.

There were people still in the room. But they were passed out on the floor.

Another effect of too much drinking and too many drugs.

She stared at them a minute, searching for any sign of movement.

She saw none.

She opened the door farther. Saw more people. Saw that they were also passed out.

Cady slipped from the office and carefully closed the door behind her.

She stared at the scene one more time.

Everyone appeared to be sleeping. Now she just had to get past them without waking anyone.

Carefully, she stepped over each person. Her heart lurched for each of them. Most were just searching for belonging. Were looking for an escape from their pain. They'd found the belonging through DH-7. They'd found the escape through drugs.

But there were so many better ways. Cady had no room to talk. She tried to escape so many things—her past. The assumptions people made about her because of her family. She filled up her loneliness with work. She had her own crutches she needed to overcome before she could judge others.

Just as she reached the door on the other side of the room, it flew open.

She jumped back, but quickly corrected her expression, morphing it from surprised to dazed.

She raked a hand through her hair and scowled before stumbling slightly on her feet.

"Can you turn off the light?" she muttered. "It's so bright out there."

Raul stood there, studying her. "I didn't know you were here tonight."

"You didn't see me?" She squinted again and ducked her head, trying to appear hungover.

"I guess I was having too much fun."

Cady shrugged. "I guess you were."

Raul took her arm. "I'm glad I found you. I want to show you something."

Fear rippled up her spine. "What's that?"

"We've been working on a new formula for flakka for years. I think we've finally got it."

"We?" she asked.

He shrugged. "Some people who work for me." He said "work" with a sardonic catch in his voice.

"I see." But she didn't. What did that mean? Was he blackmailing someone?

"Maybe you'd like to be one of the first test subjects."

She shuddered at the thought. That was the last thing she wanted. "Can I at least get over this hangover first?"

His cold eyes bored into hers. "I suppose. Meet me in the morning. We'll talk then."

She nodded. "Of course."

But she planned on getting out of here. Tonight, if possible. Tomorrow at the latest.

CHAPTER
TWENTY-SEVEN

TODAY'S GOALS: STOP TY FROM
BEING TRANSPORTED.
CONFRONT BOZEMAN. LIVE TO
TELL ABOUT IT.

CASSIDY HEADED to the police station the next day at eight a.m. sharp—right after she called Agent Peterson, who promised to get here as soon as he could.

Cassidy didn't want to risk Bozeman taking Ty away, and she would stake out the place to ensure that didn't happen.

Once there, she climbed from her sedan and headed toward the front door. Before she reached it, Jimmy James stepped from the station. The man worked at the docks, was well over six feet tall, and had meaty, tattoo-covered arms that were as big as Christmas hams.

He smiled affably, which always perplexed Cassidy. The man was a mixture of doofus and criminal, yet he was still likeable somehow.

Cassidy didn't really want to talk to him now—she wanted to see Ty, to confirm he was okay. Yet Jimmy James stopped, looking as if he had all the time in the world to catch up and like he thought they were old friends.

"Hey, Cass," he said. "Heard you stopped by my place the other day."

"How'd you know?" She hadn't exactly left a note.

"My neighbor saw you."

Cassidy didn't realize that many people would recognize her. "I did stop by, but I think I figured out my problem already. Speaking of which . . .why are you here?"

That was what she really wanted to know. Was it related to Ty's case? Totally separate? Maybe she was grasping at straws here. Or looking for any smidgen of hope she could find.

"Oh, yeah—it's fine. I needed to share something . . . with a cop." He bobbed his head up and down, sounding entirely too casual and slightly clueless.

"Do you mind if I ask what?" Time was ticking away, and she wanted to see Ty.

"Well, I heard about Ty," he said, his voice sounding deep and nasal. "He's my bud, you know. He's looked out for me on more than one occasion. When I heard what happened, I knew I had to help, if I could."

"How did you do that exactly?" Cassidy's pulse pounded with anticipation. She hoped this truly was useful, and that she wasn't getting her hopes up for nothing. With Jimmy James, nothing was certain.

"I was at that costume party down at the pier that night when everything went down. But I left early." He shifted. "I had some business to take care of."

In other words, something illegal.

"Okay . . ." Cassidy said, impatient as she waited for him to continue.

"Anyway, I left right after Chief Bozeman did. I thought it was weird because he stopped on the side of the road and picked this guy up. Then they kept driving toward The Preserve."

Cassidy heart sped. Was this the evidence they'd been looking for? It wouldn't close the case, but the information would certainly help prove their point.

"Is that right?" She tried to sound calm, but on the inside her stomach was doing cartwheels.

"Yeah, for sure. It all happened that night. Ty did not go to The Preserve."

She nodded, resisting the urge to hug the man. "Who did you tell this information to?"

"Quinton. Why?"

"Just curious. Thank you, Jimmy James."

"Any time."

As much as Cassidy wanted to see Ty, she went by Quinton's office first. She stepped inside and, before he could ask questions, closed the door.

"Well, if it isn't Katniss." He looked up from some paperwork and smiled. "I was just about to call you."

"What's up?" Cassidy wanted to both throttle the man and give him a pat on the back.

He stood and leaned closer, his normal flirtatious undertones gone. "I looked into that gun, just like you asked. It turns out the chief did send it in to be tested.

However—and this is the kicker—he didn't show anyone the reports."

"Why is that interesting?" The way things worked around here, that could be normal. Cassidy couldn't figure out the inner workings of this place.

Quinton's eyebrows shot up as he began his big reveal. "Because that gun was used in an armed robbery on the island four years ago."

Cassidy's heart skipped a beat. "Is that right?"

"That means that gun could have been planted. But, if so, whoever planted that gun first had to get into our evidence locker."

She pulled her thoughts together, nodding as each new detail kicked into place. "And when you combine that with what Jimmy James just told you, there's only one obvious answer."

Quinton frowned and rubbed his jaw. "The chief."

"Exactly. You can't let him transfer Ty today. You know that, right?"

"I'm starting to have my doubts. At first, I was convinced your boyfriend was guilty. Now I'm not sure. I'll see what I can do."

"Please. I know you don't want to be implicated in this."

His eyes widened. "You think I could be?"

She shrugged. "Bozeman has some people in his pocket. There's a chance of it."

Quinton didn't say anything, instead he seemed to be mulling over the idea.

When Cassidy stepped back out into the lobby area, she was surprised to see Vivian sitting behind the receptionist desk.

"Oh, if it isn't you! I remember you from the Friends of the Library sale." Vivian smiled warmly. "What brings you here? Are you signing up to volunteer here as well? Once volunteering is in your blood, you just can't stop yourself."

"I should consider that, but I'm actually here because a friend is locked up," Cassidy said. "I was hoping to visit him. I didn't realize you volunteered here."

"I only fill in on occasion when Margie can't come in," she said. "Today, one of her grandbabies is sick, so she's staying home to take care of the little tyke."

"Good for her. Family is important."

"Yes, family is very important." She tilted her head, something unspoken and burdensome in her eyes. It was like the words had triggered something in her.

"Is everything okay?" Cassidy's mental timer ticked away, but she asked the question anyway.

Vivian shrugged and straightened a stack of papers. "I know I shouldn't say this—you're such a good listener, though."

"What's going on?"

"It's just that . . . I've just been so worried about Alan lately." A fisted hand covered her mouth, as if it pained her to say the words. Her cheerfulness vanished, replaced with an unmistakable heaviness.

"Because of his grandmother?"

She moved her hand, revealing a deep frown. "He's just so distracted and won't open up to me."

"I'm sorry. That must be frustrating." And Bozeman probably wasn't opening up because he was involved in illegal activities. It wasn't something you necessarily went home and talked to your spouse about.

Vivian released her breath and glanced at Cassidy. "Anyway, you said you were hoping to visit our guest?"

Guest was a funny way of describing an inmate, but Cassidy would go with it. She liked the way that word sounded better. "That's right."

"I'll let you back." She grabbed her keys. "I'm not supposed to, but they're so understaffed here that I think Alan will understand. I believe you only have ten minutes, and you do know that cameras will monitor you, in case you do anything illegal, right?"

"I do." Cassidy followed her toward the door, trying to keep pace with her short, quick steps across the lobby. "Is your husband coming in today?"

"Yes, he had a busy night. He was here at the office most of the time. I told him to take a shower and get a bite to eat, that we could hold down the fort for a while."

"He sounds lucky to have a wife like you."

"We all have to look out for each other." Vivian

paused by the door and used a card to open it. "Here you go. Don't forget. Ten minutes!"

CHAPTER
TWENTY-EIGHT

CASSIDY RUSHED toward Ty's holding cell, her heart squeezing at the sight of him. At the realization that the justice system prevented her from being with the man she loved—possibly in more than one way. Because even if they got out of this, their future would be difficult considering her undercover work.

But difficult didn't mean impossible.

Ty stood from the bench, his skin pale and his body stiff.

Her heart ached at the sight. This was beginning to wear him down, wasn't it? Situations like these could break the strongest of persons.

"Cassidy . . . you're here early." His eyes flickered with discernment. "What's up?"

"I wanted to get here before Bozeman tried to have you transferred. Did he say when this was happening?"

"Probably around lunchtime."

She reached for his hand and squeezed it. "You can't go with him."

"I don't know how to stop it without making things worse. If I try to run I really will be guilty of a crime."

"We've got to think of something." Cassidy studied him, noting that his jaw looked swollen and that he cringed slightly when he moved his shoulder a certain way. "What happened to you?"

She felt sick to her stomach as the words left her lips.

"My 'roommate' last night had a vendetta. Said someone paid him to come here just to beat me up and to tell me you were in danger."

Cassidy gasped, and her concern turned to anger. "Are you okay?"

"I'm fine." His jaw flexed as his ego interceded. No Navy SEAL wanted anyone to feel sorry for him. When it came to having a man card, a SEAL's was undeniable.

"Did you report him?"

"Quinton saw it happen," Ty said. "It didn't matter. They let the man go this morning."

"Oh, Ty. I'm so sorry." Cassidy had given up everything to work in this system. Why was it failing her now? Not *just* failing her. It was *drastically* failing her. Her palms hit the jail bars and gripped them. She leaned forward, her body bent with emotion. "Why is someone doing this?"

"To make sure they're not charged with the murder of Cullum McGrath."

"By burning down your house? By sending criminals in here to beat you up? What does any of this prove?"

"Someone's trying to send a message," he said.

Cassidy lowered her voice. "We're nearly certain Bozeman is behind this. The problem is . . . we just don't have any proof that Bozeman is the bad guy. Jimmy James did tell me that he saw Bozeman pull into The Preserve that night of the crime. And that gun that was found in your house came from the evidence locker here. We're getting closer. We just need more time."

"What you don't have is motive. Why do you think he would have killed Cullum?"

"We think—are theorizing, at least—that maybe Bozeman had some debt," Cassidy said. "His grand-mother's medications—even with copays—are appar-ently burdensome. Mac said Cullum was a bookie."

"Bozeman does play poker once a week."

Adrenaline rushed through her. "Then maybe that's it. Maybe that's the last piece of information we need. Do you know who he plays with?"

Ty named a few guys.

"Maybe I'll talk to them. See what I can find out." She reached through the bars and swept Ty's hair away from his face. "I love you, Ty."

"I love you too, Cassidy. I'm sorry you have to see me like this."

"You shouldn't be behind bars. This isn't justice."

"Promise me that you won't blow your cover for me."

She opened her mouth, wanting to promise him just that. But she couldn't. She'd do anything to help him.

"Cassidy . . ."

Moisture filled her eyes again. "I can't make any guarantees."

"I need to know you'll be safe."

"Ty . . . I'm not going to let you take the fall for a crime you didn't commit."

"And I won't be able to live with myself if something happens to you because of me. Promise me."

She nibbled on the inside of her lip, her heart twisting hundreds of different ways.

"Cassidy . . ."

She wanted to promise him. Yet she didn't. She wanted to tell the truth. Yet she knew Ty wouldn't let her leave here without her word.

"I'm going to find a way to fix this." She took a step back. "And keep my identity a secret."

"Cass . . ."

She backed up before he could say anything else. "And I'm not letting you get in that car with Bozeman."

"How do you plan on doing that?"

"I don't know, but I'll think of a way."

———

Cassidy stepped outside the police station, found a patch of shade, and pulled out her phone. She had some calls to make. The first one was to give Mac an update. She feared waking him since he'd gotten in late last night after hitting traffic on the way home from Maryland. But he sounded alert.

"Do you know anything about a poker game Bozeman plays in each week?" she asked him.

Could that be the evidence they needed to nail him? She hoped so.

"I sure do. I know a couple of guys who play with him. I'll give them a call and see if they know anything about Bozeman being in debt. I doubt Vivian would allow that."

"Maybe Vivian doesn't know." The woman seemed so sweet and innocent.

"I did hear the two were living separate lives. She likes to go up and visit her sister in Jersey every chance she gets. Maybe things aren't so cheery on the home front."

Vivian had hinted that maybe they had problems. "Why do they stay together?"

"As you know, his dad is a state senator. I think Vivian likes the prestige of attending events with his family—and Bozeman probably knows he better keep the good thing he's got. But that's all speculation, of course."

"I can't let Bozeman leave with Ty, Mac."

"I agree—you can't let Bozeman take him. I fear we'll have another Elsa situation on our hands if you do. When he gets back, see if you can figure out a way to stop him from leaving."

"I'll do my best."

"See what you can find out, okay?" Maybe the

answers could be found somewhere in the space between the what-ifs.

"I'm on it. I'm leaving Ernestine's house now."

"Why are you there?" she asked.

"I stopped by to talk to Clem. He happened to be here, doing a follow-up medical visit."

"Is she okay?"

"She seems to be recovering just fine." He paused. "Be careful, Cassidy."

Everyone kept saying that. As her injuries ached again, she remembered they had good reason to be concerned. "I will be. I'm not leaving the police station."

As she said the words, Bozeman pulled up. Cassidy slunk behind the building, not ready for a confrontation. Not yet. She needed to be patient and wait for NCSBI to arrive.

She just hoped he got here in time.

CASSIDY FELT beside herself as she waited. Nothing was happening. Agent Peterson hadn't arrived. Bozeman hadn't tried to leave. And Cassidy was stuck in limbo.

Until she saw a familiar truck pull up. Mac.

He parked on the side of the police station and rushed to join Cassidy as she stood watch outside the building.

"I talked to my friends," he said, not bothering with formalities. "Bozeman has never given any indication that he's in debt."

Cassidy released a long breath—one full of disappointment. It was their one chance of getting more evidence and sealing the deal. They had means. They had opportunity. But they needed a reason for Bozeman to do this.

"If he's not in debt, why would he have killed

Cullum?" She'd turned it over and over again, but still had no solid clues.

"I have no idea," Mac said. "But he has to be trying to cover up something."

Cassidy glanced at her watch. With every minute that passed, her worry grew. "He should be bringing Ty out at any time. And the agent is late."

"He's at the mercy of the ferry system." Mac paused. "How do you plan on stopping Bozeman if he tries to leave first?"

"I really don't know. Do you have any ideas?"

Mac glanced around the corner at Bozeman's car. "It looks like it's a nonissue right now."

What? Cassidy followed his gaze. Sure enough, someone had parked behind Bozeman, essentially blocking him in. "That car looks familiar."

"It does," Mac said. "Is it—"

"It's mine," someone said, emerging from around the corner.

"Ernestine?" Cassidy blinked in surprise.

"You left your house?" Mac said.

The woman looked skittish and pale, and her gaze continually wandered the perimeter of the parking lot. "I had no choice."

"I thought you didn't leave your house? Ever?" Yet she'd left to come here? To block the chief in?

"I don't." Ernestine frowned. "Usually. But I feel terrible about what I did to you. With the journal and all."

Irritation pinched Cassidy's spine as she remembered the woman's loose lips. "Okay."

Ernestine glanced around again. "I shouldn't have done that. I just want to know so badly who killed my friend. I saw that journal as an opening to get more information and to stir the pot. I'm so sorry. I didn't consider your feelings enough."

What was done was done. There were more important matters to talk about now. "What are you doing here?"

"I just wanted to help. I overheard Clem and Mac talking, and I knew you all were here. I couldn't let what happened to Elsa happen to Ty also. I couldn't let Bozeman get away with murder. So I blocked him in. People will think I'm just a crazy old lady."

"Who attacked you, Ernestine?" Cassidy asked.

She drew in a shallow breath. "I don't know. I didn't see anything. I was standing in my kitchen one minute. The next thing I knew, someone shoved me. I fell, hit my head, and everything went black. When I woke up, the paramedics were there."

"I'm glad you're okay." Cassidy remembered finding her. She'd thought the worst, at first. And, as cranky as she might be with the woman, she didn't wish her ill. "Does anyone else have a key to your place?"

If there was no sign of forced entry, then that was the next logical choice.

"Elsa did. She was the only one."

"Did anyone find her keys after she passed?" Mac

squinted with thought. "Could someone have stolen them?"

Ernestine shook her head quickly—too quickly—and then shrugged helplessly. "You know, now that you mention it, I'm not sure. That's a good question. I never even thought about it."

"Because there's a chance the killer found them. I just don't understand why he would attack you. What could he possibly gain by doing that?" Cassidy desperately wanted to make sense of things, and mark this case closed.

"Maybe this person thought I know more than I actually do." Ernestine's rambling gaze met Cassidy's. "They could have killed me."

"Maybe."

"Until you recover from your fall, I don't think you should be here," Mac said. "You should go home."

The franticness returned. "I can't leave the two of you to take the blame."

"We'll figure something out." Cassidy placed her hand on Ernestine's arm, trying to calm her. "I agree with Mac. Being here won't help you recover. We don't want any more casualties."

"I want to do whatever I can."

"Please then. Just go home for now," Mac said.

"There's one other thing," Ernestine said. "Those cuts over your heart. I remembered where I heard about them."

Cassidy stepped closer. "Where?"

"I read about them in one of my mystery novels. It was the calling card of a serial killer."

Cassidy's throat tightened. "That's good to know."

She wasn't sure how it fit—or if it even did. But Cassidy would keep that in mind.

"Ernestine, we need to get you out of here," Mac said again. "I don't want you here when any confrontations go down. It's not what you need on your first outing in eight years."

Finally, Ernestine nodded, though she still looked hesitant. "O . . . okay then. I'm . . . sorry. At least maybe I slowed down Bozeman."

"We'll handle it," Mac said. "You take care of yourself."

"I'm leaving my car here."

Cassidy tossed the woman her keys. "That's . . . fine. Take my car, and I'll pick it up later."

Just as Ernestine scurried away, the door opened. Bozeman stepped out, leading a handcuffed Ty in front of him.

Cassidy braced herself for how things were about to play out.

Most likely, they were about to get ugly.

———

"What are you two doing out here?" Bozeman stared at Cassidy and Mac in disgust and surprise.

Cassidy stepped in front of the chief, her hands on

her hips and unyielding determination in her gaze. "You're not taking Ty anywhere."

Ty pulled away from the chief, his steady gaze silently soaking in the conversation. His body went stiff, as if on guard.

Bozeman chuckled. "I don't think that choice is yours."

"You might be surprised."

Bozeman glanced at his car. "You blocked me in? I could have you arrested."

"I did not block you in," Cassidy corrected. "That's not my vehicle."

His gaze went to Mac.

"And neither did I," Mac said drily, adding in an eye roll.

Bozeman's face reddened. "Someone better tell me what's going on here . . ."

Cassidy glanced at Ty, and he nodded, indicating he was okay. Probably the best thing he could do right now was to stay quiet, especially since he was already in hot water.

"We know you killed Cullum," Cassidy announced, diverting Bozeman from his initial concerns.

"I did what?" Bozeman's voice lilted with surprise. "You're out of your mind. Why would I kill Cullum McGrath?"

"That's what we'd like to know." Mac planted his loafer-clad feet on the sidewalk, reminding Cassidy of a sheriff in the Old West preparing for a showdown.

Bozeman narrowed his eyes. "You're in on this too? I

should have known. You've had it in for me since the day I started here at the department."

"Now, that's not true," Mac said. "I've tried to stay back and give you space."

"You've been in the peanut gallery," Bozeman growled.

"Right now, this is about you." Mac put his hands on his hips, his words and his gaze cool. "There's no need to divert the subject to me."

Cassidy had other, more pressing matters to address at the moment. "Why didn't you tell me Ed Kyle had escaped custody, Chief Bozeman? That seems like something I should have been made aware of."

His cheeks turned red again. "I was about to. But I was busy . . . putting out fires. It slipped my mind."

"What kind of fires?" Mac asked.

Bozeman seemed to realize what he'd said and snapped back into defensive mode. "It's personal, and I don't have to explain myself to you. Now, I'm taking Ty to the county jail. And blocking my car isn't going to stop me."

Bozeman jerked Ty toward the back of the building, where there was a fenced off area, usually reserved for oversized evidence or confiscated vehicles.

Confiscated vehicles . . . was that what he was going for?

Ty shot her a look. "Cassidy, it's okay."

"It's not okay. None of this is okay. We're not going to let you take him anywhere." The hardness that edged into Cassidy's voice surprised even her.

At the fence, Bozeman turned and glared at her. "Just try and stop me. I'll have you arrested."

"An agent from the North Carolina State Bureau of Investigation is on his way," Cassidy blurted. "We're telling him everything."

"What could you possibly have to tell him?"

"We know the gun that was planted at Ty's house is from the evidence locker here at the station," Cassidy announced.

Bozeman flinched. "What? Don't be ridiculous."

Again, he looked truly surprised. But Bozeman being surprised didn't add up. It didn't fit with what they knew.

"You heard me," Cassidy said.

His chest seemed to inflate again, and his chin rose as his thoughts visibly computed. "How do you know that?"

"I had someone check."

"One of my guys?"

"That's not important."

His cheeks turned red again as his temper flared. "You're turning my guys against me?"

"Apparently you had the report the whole time and didn't share it with anyone."

"I never saw that report! And I don't appreciate you inserting yourself into my investigation."

"I'm trying to find a killer," Cassidy said.

Bozeman nudged Ty. "We've got the killer. I know that's hard to accept."

"How would Ty have gotten that gun from your

evidence locker?" Mac asked. "You know it's not possible, Bozeman. You need to think a little more rationally here."

Doubt crossed his features. "You're bluffing. That gun wasn't from my police station."

"We're not bluffing," Mac said. "We have a witness that puts you at The Preserve that night."

"I did go there," he finally said. "But I didn't kill the man."

"What were you doing then?" Cassidy was anxious to hear what he had to say, how he'd try to talk his way out of this.

His shoulders slumped. "Cullum had been harassing my wife. He was a punk. I just wanted to have a little talk with him."

"In the woods?" Mac asked. "At dusk?"

"I wanted privacy. I know how Elsa's journal made it sound. But your boyfriend here was also dressed like a cop."

"We all know it wasn't Ty Elsa saw at The Preserve," Mac said. "It was you. And now you're trying to cover it up."

"Look, I admit that I didn't want people to know. I knew how it would look. But I didn't do this. I would never kill someone."

His story wasn't making sense, Cassidy mused. The ends weren't all matching. "What about the gunshot Elsa heard?"

Bozeman pressed his lips together before saying, "I saw a snake, if you must know. And I shot it. That was the shot Elsa heard. It wasn't me killing Cullum. I left him in the woods so he could find his way back on his own—maybe that wasn't nice. But he was alive when I left him."

His story might be true, but it seemed like a stretch, and Cassidy wasn't ready to believe him yet.

"All the evidence is stacking up," Mac said. "Who else could have planted that gun?"

"Another one of my officers maybe? Did you ever consider that?" Bozeman furrowed his brows and shot them a pointed look.

"As a matter of fact, we did," Mac said. "And we cleared them. We just haven't been able to clear you."

He huffed and pushed Ty toward the fence. "I've had enough of this conversation. I'm taking him to the county jail now."

"No, you're not." Cassidy stepped forward, ready to do whatever it took to stop him.

"Why are you so opposed to me taking him?"

"Because I'm afraid you'll kill him."

Bozeman's eyes widened again, and he let out a chortle. "You really think I would do that?"

"Without Ty around to defend himself, you'll be home free," Cassidy said. "You'll literally get away with murder."

His eyes narrowed. "Who are you? You have more guts than anyone I've ever met before. There's more to you than you let on."

"My parents always said I was a fighter," Cassidy

said. "And that's what I am. I'm fighting for the man I love."

"That's sweet, but you're too late. You should have stopped him before he killed Mr. McGrath."

"He had no reason."

"When you have PTSD, you don't need a reason."

"We know about your trips to Raleigh," Cassidy said. "You say you're taking care of your grandmother, but my guess is that you're going somewhere else . . . to gamble. Maybe you're in debt for some reason."

"My grandmother? My grandparents have all been dead for probably five years now. Where in the world did you get that information?"

"From your wife," Cassidy said, a nagging doubt tugged at the back of her mind.

Before she could fully identify it, she sensed a shadow behind her.

"YOU JUST COULDN'T LET it go, could you, Cassidy?" Vivian stepped from the back door of the building, a gun in her hands and a crazy look in her eyes.

"Vivian, no . . ." Bozeman's face crumpled with disbelief and sadness. "What are you doing out here? Get back inside. And put that gun down."

Vivian didn't seem to hear him. Instead, she sneered at Cassidy, the gun trembling in her hands. "You just had to keep pushing. If you'd let it go, none of us would be in this situation right now."

Vivian was behind this? Could that be correct?

Cassidy needed more time to think this through.

Bozeman raised his hands in a peaceful gesture and took a step closer. "You don't want to do this, Vivian."

"Yes, I do," she snapped, turning her wild eyes on her husband. "I have to. I have to keep everyone quiet so life as we know it can go on."

Cassidy wasn't sure, but she didn't think Bozeman had any clue about this. He looked and acted just as surprised as everyone else. And that realization left her feeling temporarily off-balance.

"What does that mean, Vivian?" The corners of Bozeman's eyes seemed to turn downward along with his lips. "So life as we know it can go on?"

"You know what it means. It means I got bored while you were working all the time." Vivian's nostrils flared, and her sweet demeanor disappeared in a vapor. "I started playing some games online. Then I went up to visit my sister, and I swung by that casino near Ocean City. It was . . . fun."

In her manic state, she'd begun to gamble . . . which had no doubt led to multiple other problems.

Cassidy glanced at Bozeman again and could tell that he already knew this part of the story. She waited to see how everything else would play out.

"I did well at first," Vivian continued. "And then I started losing. I thought I could make the money back. I just needed a couple of good wins. But it didn't happen."

"So you connected with Cullum," Cassidy muttered, some of the pieces fitting together. "But you couldn't pay him back, so he came down here to find you."

"He demanded his money, but I didn't have it. I didn't know what to do."

"I told you I took care of him," Bozeman said, his face moist as reality kicked in. "I paid him off, and he was going to go away. What did you do?"

Vivian swung the gun around, its barrel bobbing at each of them. "I followed you through the woods. I saw you pay him off. But I knew that wasn't the end of it. I had to do more. He was wandering around, looking lost. I decided to talk to him. Tell him how he'd messed up my life. He didn't like that. So I shot him in the chest. All of those shooting lessons you gave me really paid off."

"Vivian . . ." Bozeman rocked his head from side to side. "No . . ."

"I didn't want you to be blamed. I knew Elsa had seen you go into the woods, and I thought she might have reported it. So I went back the next morning. I brought a Ziploc bag and put the contents of Cullum's wallet inside. People do that at the beach sometimes. I added the note from Ty. I had a sample of his hand-writing from when we asked people here in town to recommend their favorite novels for a feature we were doing at the library."

"So you forged it." Bozeman frowned.

"I knew it would disappoint you."

"We could have gotten through it," Bozeman said. "There are better ways, Vivian. You know that."

Her nostrils flared again, and that crazy look kicked up a notch. "It's too late now. Everything has been set in motion. You need to take him to the county jail. He'll have an accident on the way there. He'll try to attack you, and you'll have no choice but to defend yourself."

"That won't be happening," Cassidy said.

Vivian's eyes threw daggers at her as she turned the

gun on Cassidy. "I didn't ask your opinion! You've already messed all of this up!"

"You volunteer here at the station, don't you?" Cassidy said. "That's how you had access to the evidence locker. You took the gun and planted it in Ty's house."

"That stupid police radio is always on at the house. When I heard the body had been found, I knew it was time to snap into action."

"How'd you break into my house?" Ty asked. He'd been silently observing it all.

She shrugged. "My husband's a police officer. I've learned a few things over the years. All I had to do was give your dog a steak, and he didn't bother me a bit. I also put the keys in your truck."

"And set his house on fire last night," Cassidy added.

"I needed to get you off my case." Vivian glowered, obviously unstable.

"Then you sent that man to hurt me?" Cassidy questioned. "You really were desperate. I just don't know how you could afford him—although, this does help to explain how he got away."

"His name is Ed. He's an old friend."

"Ed Kyle is actually Ed Stephens?" Bozeman barked. "Your old high school boyfriend who's been locked up more times than I can count? Have you been seeing him?"

Vivian's face twisted with anger and frustration. "No, he's just been helping me. He moved to Nags

Head not long ago, and we ran into each other when I worked the seafood festival there."

"Why wouldn't you tell me that?" Bozeman's voice dropped with disappointment . . . and maybe betrayal. "He's nothing but trouble."

"I needed someone who was trouble!" Vivian's nostrils flared. "You wouldn't have the nerve to do what was necessary."

"Vivian . . ."

"Did you take the bomb from the evidence locker also?" Cassidy asked, eyeballing Vivian's gun and considering how to get it from her. That was the one thing that didn't make sense. A bomb had been planted on a ferry last month. That was why Cassidy had been certain there was a dirty cop.

"I did. I met someone who asked me to do it. I needed the money." Vivian pointed the gun at all of them again. "Now, before anyone sees us, you need to get in the car, Alan. Take him with you."

"That's not going to help anything here," Bozeman said, moving in front of Ty. "I'm not going to kill Mr. Chambers."

"You don't have a choice. It's the only way. Can't you see that?" Her voice cracked with crazy.

Suddenly, it made sense. It wasn't Bozeman's grandma he was taking care of—she wasn't the one losing her mind. It was *Vivian*. She must have had some kind of mental break. Like that Olympian who became an escort. A mix of medications and wrong mental diagnosis, and the person seemingly went off the deep end.

"Vivian . . ." Bozeman took another step closer.

"I don't want to shoot you too." The gun trembled in her hands.

"We're not going to get out of this unscathed. We might as well face the music. Together. I'll be with you."

Vivian's eyes were getting crazier by the moment. "Just do it! Get in the car with Ty or I'll pull this trigger. Don't test me!"

All of a sudden, a strange sound came from the other side of the police station.

Everyone turned just as a big pink truck charged toward them, "When the Saints Go Marching In" blaring from its tinny speakers.

Elsa.

Cassidy gasped, her gaze swerving to the driver's seat.

Ernestine was behind the wheel.

The sight of Elsa stunned everyone long enough for Bozeman to grab Vivian's gun, tuck it into his waistband, and subdue her with a bear hug.

Mac jumped into Elsa, stopping the truck before it hit anyone.

Cassidy rushed toward Ty, slipping an arm around his waist and wishing desperately she could get these handcuffs off him. Since she couldn't, she'd be by his side in case he needed her.

"You killed my friend!" Ernestine shouted at Vivian as she stepped out of the truck. "Why? Why did you kill Elsa?"

Mac kept a hand on her arm, as if holding her back from doing something stupid.

"She saw me come out of the woods that night," Vivian said. "She was going to start putting things together. I couldn't let that happen. I had to preserve my life here. I had to."

"Hon, you need help," Bozeman said.

"I had no choice. I had to do these things. Can't you see?"

At that moment, a vehicle with NCSBI emblazoned on the side pulled up. Agent Peterson was here. And the chief wouldn't be able to deny the evidence now.

Bozeman looked at Cassidy, then Mac and Ty. Grief was etched into his face. "I'm . . . I'm sorry for everything that happened. I had no idea."

Cassidy might have this mystery behind her, but she felt a strange sense of sadness and compassion for the man she'd once suspected.

CHAPTER
THIRTY-ONE

TWO HOURS LATER, Ty stepped out of the door leading to the holding cell area.

He was a free man.

With Ricco's help, the magistrate had expedited the process of his release.

Cassidy ran toward him and propelled herself into his embrace. He lifted her off the ground, his arms wrapping around her.

He held her. Squeezed her. Acted like he didn't want to let her go either.

When he finally did release her, he planted a firm kiss on her lips, the kind of kiss that made her spine turn to gel.

"I've been dreaming about doing this for three days now," he murmured in her ear. "It felt like three years."

She looked up at his handsome face and smiled. "You and me both."

As a footfall sounded behind them, they pulled away.

Bozeman stood there. Gone was the usual arrogance in his gaze, and he shifted uncomfortably. The NCSBI had probably talked to him already, but no doubt they'd have more questions. Mac was giving his statement now.

"I think I owe you both an apology," he started. "I had no idea what Vivian was up to."

Cassidy kept an arm at Ty's waist as she turned toward Bozeman, waiting to hear what else he had to say.

"A year ago, she had a miscarriage. It devastated her," Bozeman explained. "I'd always seen some signs in her of a mental imbalance, I guess you'd call it. But after she lost the baby, she was off the charts. I took her to the doctor, and he put her on meds. But Vivian didn't like them. She'd act like she was taking them, but she wouldn't really."

"It sounds tough," Ty said, compassion in his voice.

"It was. And, unfortunately, it was easier for me to pour myself into my work than it was to watch her like that. I just had no idea she would take it this far. I knew she'd gambled some online. And I knew Cullum had come into town for her."

"What happened at The Preserve then?" Ty asked.

"I met Cullum there and paid my wife's debt. I thought that was the end of it. But Vivian apparently followed me. She snuck through the woods—coming in from the other side where I wouldn't see her. She shot him with a gun she got from the evidence locker here and took the money back. She gambled some more with it. Apparently, we're up to one hundred thousand in debt now."

Cassidy blanched at the amount. She couldn't even imagine.

"I didn't know what she was capable of," Bozeman continued. "She said she got some ideas from those mystery novels, even setting up the sound of a dog barking in a burning house to lure you in and having Ed cut the X over your heart."

Cassidy had to wonder if the chief had at least suspected something. Or had he really turned a blind eye to it all? Had he been in denial?

"She's . . . clever." To say the least, Cassidy thought.

"She gave up the location of Ed Kyle," Bozeman continued. "Quinton is on his way over to arrest him. Again, I'm sorry. I'm going to get her the help she needs. And, of course, she'll have to do the time."

"What about you?" Ty asked. "What are you going to do?"

"I've already decided to resign. Let's face it—I was never cut out for this line of work. I'm going to go work for my father."

"The senator?" Cassidy asked. Politics seemed like just the right place for someone so incompetent.

"The move will be best for everyone." He stared at Cassidy. "That also means there will be a job opening here."

She shrugged and pointed to herself. "Me? Oh, I'm not police chief material."

"I hate to say it, but you are. You really are. You should think about it. My gut feeling is that Mac will fill in until someone permanent is hired."

"I appreciate the vote of confidence." He had no idea, though.

Agent Dan Peterson with the NCSBI stepped into their conversation. "We're going to need to get statements from you two."

"Of course," Cassidy said.

And she could stay quiet about who she really was. Pretend she was just a victim or a citizen vigilante.

With their arms wrapped around each other still, Cassidy and Ty followed Agent Peterson into his temporary office.

Cassidy felt forever grateful that things had worked out. Because they could have turned out so much worse.

CASSIDY LEANED INTO TY, her back resting against his chest as they sat in front of the beachside bonfire. His arms circled her waist, pulling her close, and she tucked herself into him.

The sky was inky black above them, and the waves thundered onto the shore. Pinpricks of lights peeked through the darkness, seeming to sprinkle favor on them.

For now.

Cassidy knew all too well how things could change as quickly as the tide.

The whole gang had come over to her place as an impromptu welcome-home party for Ty. Mac and Clemson had also joined them, as well as a few others. They had a cookout, and, for dessert, everyone had ice cream from Elsa.

Surprisingly, no one minded eating it now that they knew the ice cream truck wasn't haunted.

The gathering had been nice, an answer to prayer.

"You know, I actually kind of felt sorry for Bozeman," Ty said, his breath tickling her ear. "He looked totally stunned when Vivian stepped outside with the gun."

Cassidy couldn't stop thinking about it. "He did. He had no idea things were this much out of control with Vivian. And her actions scream of betrayal. I know she's fighting some mental issues, but that's still got to be hard for Bozeman to swallow."

"I agree. I still think he made a horrible police chief, but he has a tough road ahead. I'll be praying for him." Ty reached over to pet Kujo, who plopped in the sand beside them.

Sometimes, the bad guy was right in front of you, and he—or she—was the person you least suspected.

"Any luck getting up with Samuel?" Ty asked.

Cassidy let her head fall back against his chest. "No, not yet."

"You're worried, aren't you?"

She drew in a breath and held it, contemplating her response. "I am. It's not like him not to respond."

"Hopefully you'll hear from him soon."

"Yeah, I hope so."

Silence stretched a moment.

Ty shifted and turned toward Cassidy. Something serious stained his gaze, something heavy on his mind. She braced herself. He'd had a lot of time to think in jail. Had he had some revelations about their relationship?

The bigger question was: Would Cassidy like any of them? Or had Ty finally figured out that Cassidy was too complicated? Anyone would be overwhelmed by the circumstances surrounding her—dating her wasn't an easy path.

"Thank you for everything you did," Ty said.

Cassidy squeezed his arm. "I wish I could have done more. Or done it faster. But I'm so glad everything turned out."

"I am too. Cassidy, I felt helpless when I was in jail, and I hated it. It brought back a lot of memories of my time in the Middle East. Of my brother. I felt like I'd been pulled out in one of those rip currents and couldn't get out."

"I understand that feeling, Ty." All too well.

His eyes searched hers, his normally teasing glimmer gone. "I don't want to feel helpless again."

His concern was touching—truly—but he couldn't worry about her so much. "Ty, I'm a detective. And I love that you're protective of me, but I've got more training than the average person."

Her words didn't seem to affect him. "I don't want to lose you."

"We learned in police academy that we can't save everyone, Ty. You need to give yourself that permission. It's okay." If something happened to her, it was because of her own choices. It had nothing to do with Ty.

"I know I can't save everyone." His voice came out raspy and deep. "You're the only one I care about."

The sincerity in his voice melted her heart. Cassidy's

gaze went to his lips, and she slipped her arms around his neck. Their lips met in a kiss. They only pulled away when Kujo started barking at them.

"Thanks, Kujo." Ty chuckled and rubbed the dog's head. "You know how to ruin a moment."

Cassidy leaned into Ty, wishing this moment never had to end. Wishing there wasn't a trial coming up. Wishing she knew who had killed Lucy. If Lucy's father was somehow involved. And the bigger question—why? If Lucy's father was involved, what could his motive possibly be?

But, for now, she'd enjoy being with Ty.

He cleared his throat, signaling another change in conversation. "I need to go home and be with my mom for a while, Cassidy."

Cassidy's heart squeezed at the emotion and under-lying message in his voice. He was concerned. So was she. "I know. I think that's a great idea."

His eyes latched onto hers, something unsaid in their depth. "I wish you could come."

"I wish I could too. But I can't leave." If Cassidy left, there was a greater chance she'd be exposed. That DH-7 would find her. She was too close to the trial for that to happen.

"I don't want to leave you." He leaned forward, burying himself in her hair.

She rested her hand against his jaw. "I know."

"You don't understand." His voice sounded husky, serious. "I don't ever want to leave you."

"That's sweet, Ty. But I can wait for you to return."

His grip around her tightened. "What I'm trying to say, Cassidy, is that I want to spend the rest of my life with you. I want to marry you, Cassidy."

Her throat tightened with emotion . . . and love . . . and exuberance. Was he saying what she thought he was saying? "Are you . . . ?"

"Proposing?" Ty smiled. "I guess I am. I didn't really plan this. I know it's not romantic like it should be and that you deserve more, better—"

"Yes."

Ty stopped, and his eyes widened. "What?"

"I want to marry you too." Tears filled Cassidy's eyes.

He released a breath, and his lips covered hers. Softly. Tentatively. And then passionately until everything else was forgotten.

When Cassidy finally pulled away, another dose of reality hit her.

"But Ty . . ." She glanced at his chest, trying to find the words. "I don't know what's going to happen. I can't get married under my new identity . . . or my old identity and—"

"We'll figure it out," he insisted.

"I wish I could promise you more." She did. She wanted to uncomplicate things. But that was impossible.

"You just promised me forever. You're just not sure how we'll get there. But I'm confident we will." His voice remained steadfast and sure.

"You're right." She smiled. "We will."

The trial was a month away. Then Cassidy would know something.

But the current around her was pulling harder, stronger by the moment. Cassidy knew clear skies weren't on the horizon for her.

Not now. But maybe soon the tide would change, and storm season would pass.

She prayed to God that would be the case . . . and soon.

~~~

Thank you for reading *Perilous Riptide*. If you enjoyed this book, please consider leaving a review.

Keep reading for a preview of *Deadly Undertow*.
~~~

DEADLY UNDERTOW: CHAPTER ONE

TODAY'S GOALS: SPEND AS MUCH TIME WITH TY AS POSSIBLE. THAT'S IT.

CASSIDY STEPPED BACK from the dining room table and smiled at what she saw.

"What do you think, Kujo?" She looked down at the golden retriever sitting beside her, his tongue hanging toward the floor like a banner proclaiming happiness.

He let out a quick but enthusiastic bark.

"You approve?" she confirmed. "You think Ty will like it?"

The dog barked again.

Cassidy patted his head, his soft fur feeling luxurious against her fingertips. "I know I can always count on you, boy."

Was this what her life had boiled down to over the past week? Talking to Ty's dog like it was a normal thing? Was she that desperate for Ty to return?

He'd been gone for seven days, visiting his mother who was having surgery. Her ovarian cancer had spread, and doctors had no choice but to operate since chemo and radiation hadn't worked. Thankfully, the surgery had gone well, and Del was now at home recovering.

Cassidy wished she could have gone with Ty. But she couldn't leave Lantern Beach—not without serious risk of blowing everything. Since the trial against members of DH-7 was only a month away, she needed to sit tight and bide her time until she could mark this chapter of her life closed.

Strangely enough, being in hiding was one of the best things that could have happened to her.

In thirty minutes, when Ty pulled into his driveway—provided he was on time—Cassidy was going to surprise him with brunch. She'd made a fruit salad, blueberry muffins, and a spinach and sausage quiche.

Just for fun, Cassidy had added a white tablecloth to cover the jaundiced wood of the old seventies-style dining room table. She'd topped the linen with some candles and the finest dishes she could find at her rental —which just happened to be old with brown flowers on the edges. The September day was beautiful—in the mid-seventies—so she'd opened her windows, and a pleasant breeze made the whole house aflutter with excitement.

In all of its imperfections, the setup still seemed simply perfect.

Outside, the sound of tires crunching against the gravel drive leading to her beach cottage caught her ear.

Ty.

Her heart surged. He was early. And Cassidy was more than okay with that.

Quickly, she ran a hand through her long blonde hair and straightened her blousy shirt.

Cassidy hadn't expected to miss Ty this much. After all, she'd always been the independent type. But Ty had gained an unmistakable place in her heart over the past few months—a place she wanted to keep him forever and always.

Kujo barked, obviously hearing the vehicle and anticipating the arrival of his owner as well.

"We both missed him, didn't we?" she murmured.

Kujo barked again, almost as if he understood every word she said. It was just one more reason she loved the canine.

Cassidy did one last check of the house, made sure everything was in place, and then listened as footsteps ascended the weathered, wooden stairs outside her beach cottage.

She started toward the door when she smelled something faint but unpleasant.

Smoke.

The quiche!

How could she have forgotten it was in the oven?

She hurried toward the kitchen and grabbed an oven mitt. As soon as Cassidy pulled the pan out, she scrunched her nose at the blackened mess in the pie dish. The recipe was ruined.

So much for the romantic breakfast she'd planned as a welcome home.

Cassidy frowned and tried to think of a quick solution.

Before she could, a knock sounded at the door. Hopefully the open windows would air the smoke from the place quickly. Otherwise, her surprise meal would be a surprise trip to the clinic for a breathing treatment.

Thankfully, Ty was the forgiving type.

Cassidy set the charred quiche in the sink and tossed a towel over it. Then she hurried across the room and threw the front door open, figuring she'd make the best of things.

But it wasn't Ty standing on the other side.

Her stomach dropped more quickly than an anchor during a squall.

It was . . . "Ryan?"

A grin lit Ryan Samson's perfectly chiseled face—a face she hadn't seen in months. Without invitation, he stepped inside with outstretched arms.

"Cad—Cassidy!" His voice rolled over her, as smooth and polished as he was. "I've missed you. And you look great. Beach life really agrees with you."

Before she realized what was happening, Ryan embraced her. His familiar scent—a spicy blend that always reminded her of the smell of money—filled her senses and took her back in time. Back to her old life. Back to the person she used to be before DH-7 had turned her life upside down.

Cassidy stiffened, her thoughts clashing inside her. She couldn't make sense of them right now, so instead she stepped back and looked at Ryan.

Ryan . . .

He was here. In Lantern Beach. After not speaking to Cassidy for nearly four months.

He hadn't changed much in the time since Cassidy had seen him last. Even though he was in a beach town, he wore a designer gray pullover and dress slacks that probably cost as much as one week's rent at some of the smaller beach cottages in the area.

He still had dark brown hair that was styled with perfection—despite the area's wind and humidity. He was clean-shaven, picture perfect, and screamed of someone with a future in politics. The camera loved him. People loved him. And he had a great record for putting away the bad guys.

Kujo sat beside Cassidy, a low growl rumbling in his chest. She patted the canine's head, trying to quietly assure him that everything was okay—okay being a relative term right now.

Cassidy stepped away from Ryan's embrace and shook her head in disbelief. "What are you doing here? I'm . . . shocked to say the least."

"What? I thought you'd be happy to see me." He shrugged, looking equal parts arrogantly offended and coolly unaffected. He'd always been the aloof type, the king of logic and level-headedness.

So much so that he'd persuaded Cassidy to keep their relationship a secret back when they'd been together in Seattle. At the time, Cassidy had convinced herself it made sense. Now . . . it just felt slimy and wrong.

"Kujo, it's okay," she murmured, trying to get the dog to stop growling before someone got hurt—that someone being Ryan.

The canine gave one last grumble before stopping to give Ryan a death stare instead.

Where did Cassidy even start this conversation? She closed the door and turned toward her ex, a sense of dread seizing her. What would have led him to find her? Whatever it was, it couldn't be good.

"How'd you find me?" She looked out the window for any signs of trouble. "Did anyone follow you here?"

Ryan let out a puff of air, combined with a deprecating chuckle. "I'll explain everything. Give me time. And of course no one followed me. I'm not stupid."

Cassidy crossed her arms, still on edge. Ryan showing up here was not normal. Or expected. Or okay.

Nor was his superior attitude.

"Why are you here? Did something happen? Didn't you get my messages?" The questions rushed out, all equally important and pressing and impossible to prioritize.

"We have a lot to talk about. I thought it was best if I came here so we could figure this out face-to-face." In one motion, he pulled Cassidy into his arms again. He stroked her back and murmured into her hair, "It's so good to see you, to hold you. I've missed you so much."

As Cassidy stiffened and tried to push away, she heard a footstep. She craned her neck to see beyond Ryan, and her fears were realized.

Ty stood at the open door—a total contrast to Ryan

in his faded jeans and flannel shirt. Ty's hair was messy, his jaw unshaven, and his eyes warm.

Picture perfect? Maybe not if you were a politician. But Ty embodied everything that Cassidy found appealing—he exuded a manliness that polished Ryan would never reach.

Kujo ran to greet him, the dog's welcome much warmer now.

The shocked and then hardened expression on Ty's face said it all. This was not the welcome he'd envisioned.

Cassidy stepped back, a rush of nerves rising in her. She liked to keep a cool head, but this was just uncomfortable . . . and unfortunate. And horrible, horrible timing all around.

She turned toward Ty, and Ryan followed her gaze. Ty's hands were on his hips, and the air crackled with awkwardness all around them.

"Ty!" She wanted to rush into his arms, but until she and Ryan talked more, that also felt awkward. Instead, Cassidy stepped forward and grabbed his arm, pulling him closer before whispering, "I'll explain all of this."

Ty's gaze went from Cassidy to Ryan and then back to Cassidy. Her words apparently didn't reassure him, and he put on what Cassidy called his "SEAL about to jump into action" face.

"What's going on?" Ty's words sounded a lot like Kujo's rumbling growl.

Ryan stepped forward, his hand outstretched like any good elected official determined to win over the favor of the masses. "I'm Ryan Samson. Pleasure to meet you."

Ty stared at his hand but didn't return the gesture. His perceptive eyes continued to study the situation. "Ty Chambers."

Ryan coolly assessed Ty.

Two alphas in one room? There was no way this would turn out well.

"Ty, I'm going to need some time alone with Cad—Cassidy." Ryan said the words like he expected everyone to listen—which was what generally happened in his life.

But not here on Lantern Beach.

Ryan was not going to step back into Cassidy's life and begin to dictate what she did and didn't do—or who came and went, for that matter.

"That's not necessary." Cassidy still held to Ty's arm. "I'd prefer that Ty be here."

Ryan narrowed his eyes as if the idea was preposterous. "Unless he's got clearance, you know the details we need to discuss are confidential."

She wanted to argue with Ryan, but she knew his words were true. What the two of them needed to talk about wasn't light or casual conversation. The details were all classified, and Cassidy had even signed a form to ensure it. In this case, she'd have to put her own desires and wishes on the back burner, like it or not.

Or not being her choice.

"Okay," Cassidy said. "I get it. But first I need to talk to Ty. Alone. Outside."

Tension built in Cassidy's chest with every second the three of them were in the same room.

Ty drew his gaze away from Ryan, his features as stony and hard as a soldier on the battlefield making the call to fight or retreat. "Of course."

Cassidy led him to the deck, away from the window, so Ryan couldn't overhear anything. As soon as she stepped outside, the sound of waves rolling in the Atlantic Ocean filled her senses. The sun hit her face. A family played Frisbee on the beach nearby.

This was her happy place.

Normally.

Right now, tension gripped her in a chokehold that made it hard to breathe.

As soon as they were far enough away, she grabbed Ty's arms, knowing she didn't have much time to get through to him, to say what she needed to say.

"Is that your ex-fiancé?" Ty started.

"Yes. I had no idea Ryan was going to come here. He literally showed up on my doorstep two minutes before you arrived."

Ty studied her gaze, his perceptive eyes absorbing everything. "Does he know you're not engaged anymore?"

"I don't know. I'd . . . . planned a breakfast for you. That's what the smoke was from . . . but that's a different story. I wanted to hear about your mom. And . . . I've missed you terribly."

Cassidy wanted to embrace him. Kiss him. Enjoy their time together.

Ty dipped his head, his eyes softening. "I've missed you too. I want to be there to hear whatever he has to say. I already know what's going on."

Her gut twisted. "But you're not supposed to know. And Ryan can't speak about the details in front of people who aren't approved. He's a by-the-rules kind of guy. You know what that's like from your days as a SEAL. It's out of my control."

She silently begged him to understand.

Ty pressed his lips together, his gaze simmering, and tension causing his jaw muscles to jump. "So I'm just supposed to go home?"

"Just for a few minutes. I'm sure Ryan won't be here long. I . . . I just don't know what's going on. He wouldn't have come unless it was important. I do know that."

Ty let out a long puff of air. He considered himself her protector—and he wouldn't let the law stand in the way of that. Yet he also respected her.

"Cassidy . . ."

She squeezed his arms again. "I know. I do. Believe me. Just let me talk to Ryan, okay? And I'm sorry. I didn't want it to be like this."

Ty glanced back at the door one last time. "You're a smart woman. I'll trust your judgment and respect your choice."

Cassidy kissed his cheek, relieved that he understood. "Thank you. I'll be over as soon as I can."

Ty nodded, but his neck looked stiff and his eyes

hard. "Kujo can stay with you to make sure your 'friend' doesn't misbehave."

Cassidy turned back to the house, unsure if she was excited to hear an update from Ryan or if she should dread it. Maybe for now she would just settle on getting this over with.

To continue reading click here

ALSO BY CHRISTY BARRITT:

BOOKS IN THE LANTERN BEACH UNIVERSE

LANTERN BEACH MYSTERIES

The series that started it all! When a notorious gang puts a bounty on Detective Cady Matthews' head, she has no choice but to hide until she can testify at trial. But her temporary home across the country on a remote North Carolina island isn't as peaceful as she initially thinks. Living under the new identity of Cassidy Livingston, she struggles to keep her investigative skills tucked away. One wrong move could lead to both her discovery and her demise.

#1 Hidden Currents

#2 Flood Watch

#3 Storm Surge

#4 Dangerous Waters

#5 Perilous Riptide

#6 Deadly Undertow

LANTERN BEACH ROMANTIC SUSPENSE

Standalone romantic suspense novels that fear a pulse-pounding story centered around beloved Lantern Beach residents.

Tides of Deception
Shadow of Intrigue
Storm of Doubt
Winds of Danger
Rains of Remorse
Torrents of Fear

LANTERN BEACH PD

When a cult moves to Lantern Beach, the whole island is in upheaval. Police Chief Cassidy Chambers must find answers before total chaos erupts.

#1 On the Lookout
#2 Attempt to Locate
#3 First Degree Murder
#4 Dead on Arrival
#5 Plan of Action

LANTERN BEACH BLACKOUT

Join a group of Navy SEALs who've come to Lantern Beach to start a private security firm. But a secret from their past may destroy them.

#1 Dark Water
#2 Safe Harbor
#3 Ripple Effect
#4 Rising Tide

LANTERN BEACH GUARDIANS

During a turbulent storm, a child is found on the beach, washed up from the ocean. Making matters worse—the girl can't speak.

#1 Hide and Seek
#2 Shock and Awe
#3 Safe and Sound

LANTERN BEACH BLACKOUT: THE NEW RECRUITS

Four new recruits join Blackout, but someone is determined to teach them a lesson.

#1 Rocco
#2 Axel
#3 Beckett
#4 Gabe

LANTERN BEACH MAYDAY

Kenzie and Jimmy James work on a luxury yacht chartering a dangerous course.

#1 Run Aground
#2 Dead Reckoning
#3 Tipping Point

LANTERN BEACH CHRISTMAS

Catch up with your favorite Lantern Beach characters as they come together to help the town's beloved police chief.

Silent Night

LANTERN BEACH BLACKOUT: DANGER RISING

A new team is formed to combat a new enemy. The mission puts everyone on the line, and failure will mean certain death.

#1 Brandon
#2 Dylan
#3 Maddox
#4 Titus

BEACH BOUND
BOOKS AND BEANS MYSTERIES

When widow Tali Robinson moves to Lantern Beach to renovate an old oceanfront store and turn it into a bookstore/coffee shop, the last thing she expects to find is a human skeleton hidden within the walls. But her troubles don't stop there, and before long she realizes she doesn't have to dig for trouble, she's bound to run into it.

#1 Bound by Murder
#2 Bound by Disaster
#3 Bound by Mystery
#4 Bound by Trouble
#5 Bound by Mayhem

ABOUT THE AUTHOR

USA Today has called Christy Barritt's books "scary, funny, passionate, and quirky."

Christy writes both mystery and romantic suspense novels that are clean with underlying messages of faith. Her books have sold more than three million copies and have won the Daphne du Maurier Award for Excellence in Suspense and Mystery, have been twice nominated for the Romantic Times Reviewers' Choice Award, and have finaled for both a Carol Award and Foreword Magazine's Book of the Year.

She is married to her Prince Charming, a man who thinks she's hilarious—but only when she's not trying to be. Christy is a self-proclaimed klutz, an avid music lover who's known for spontaneously bursting into song, and a road trip aficionado.

When she's not working or spending time with her family, she enjoys singing, playing the guitar, and exploring small, unsuspecting towns where people have no idea how accident-prone she is.

Find Christy online at:

www.christybarritt.com

www.facebook.com/christybarritt

www.twitter.com/cbarritt

Sign up for Christy's newsletter to get information on all of her latest releases here: **www.christybarritt.com/ newsletter-sign-up/**

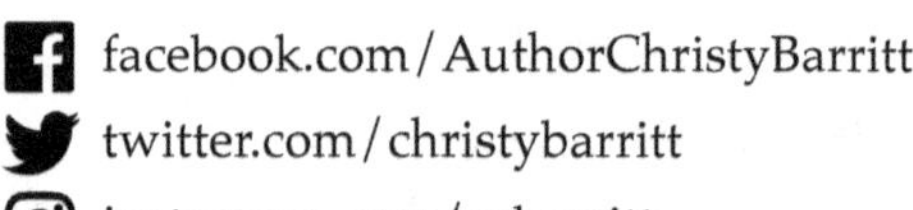

facebook.com / AuthorChristyBarritt

twitter.com / christybarritt

instagram.com / cebarritt

www.ingramcontent.com/pod-product-compliance
Lightning Source LLC
Chambersburg PA
CBHW051138130726
47988CB00005B/1885